Find You A Real One

A Friends to Lovers Romance

TANISHA STEWART

Find You A Real One: A Friends to Lovers Romance
Copyright © 2021 Tanisha Stewart

All rights reserved.

Find You A Real One: A Friends to Lovers Romance is a work of fiction. Any resemblance to events, locations, or persons living or dead is coincidental. No part of this book may be reproduced in any written, electronic, recording, or photocopying form without written permission of the author, Tanisha Stewart.

Books may be purchased in quantity and for special sales by contacting the publisher, Tanisha Stewart, at tanishastewart.author@gmail.com.

First Edition
Published in the United States of America
by Tanisha Stewart

Dear Reader,

I wrote this book while I was in high school and read it back over last year, along with a few other books I wrote during that time frame. From reading those throwback books, three separate series emerged: an enemies to lovers, which became my Phate Series, a friends to lovers, which became the Real Ones, and another series I plan to release in the near future.

It is my great hope that you enjoy reading about these characters as much as I enjoyed writing them.

Disclaimer: this story does contain graphic violence and abuse. If you are sensitive to those types of issues, this may not be the book for you.

Happy Reading!

Tanisha Stewart

Find You A Real One

A Friends to Lovers Romance

Life is all about making choices. You just have to make the right ones. If you believe you create your own reality, then you can make your life into whatever you want it to be, because it's your life.

It's your choice.

Alize (Shorty) Henderson

This life ain't nothing but a system we all get caught up in.

People say everything happens for a reason; I say nothing happens for a reason. Things happen because that was how it was supposed to be.

Good things happen to some people, and bad things happen to others. Some people try to break the cycle but give up when they realize they are stuck.

Elida Johnson

Shorty

It was a hot summer day right before the start of freshman year.
I was standing outside with my best friend, Janie. Other kids from our apartment complex were also out, some shooting each other with water guns, and others just chilling in the shade.

Me and Janie were propped up near her mom's car, trying to look cute for the boys in the neighborhood while watching some little girls play hopscotch on the sidewalk as we talked. My eyes lit up as I remembered something. "Oh! Janie, you heard about that new park that opened, Unique Amusements?"

"Yeah! We've like, so got to go!"

"Yeah, we should. It's gonna be hot."

"Yeah, and who knows how many cute guys will be there?" She winked mischievously. "Maybe even Marcus."

"Oh, yeah, I hadn't even thought about that. I hope he is there. He is super fine. Mmm, mmm, mmm!" I began to daydream about him. Marcus, a boy from our neighborhood, was the finest guy I had ever seen. I liked him since I was seven years old. He's got deep, dark, chocolate skin and hazel eyes. There was a rumor going around that he was going to ask me out. I hoped it was true. I imagined the words coming from his perfect lips, soft and full.

I only got to kiss him once during a game of Truth or Dare . . . .

"Shorty. SHORTY!" Janie was yelling for my attention.

"What?" I snapped out of my reverie.

"I said, here he comes right now." I turned and looked. Sure enough, Marcus was walking his fine self over to where we were standing, along with his best friend, Reggie.

"What up, Shorty?" Marcus gave me a hug and a stare that almost made me melt. Reggie just lifted the tip of his fitted hat and nodded.

I focused on Marcus, while Janie eyed Reggie. "Nothing. What's up with you?"

He licked his lips.

My eyelids fluttered. *Is he about to ask me out?* "Ooh boy," I said, testing the waters. "Don't do that." I flipped my freshly relaxed hair over my shoulder for emphasis.

"Do what?" He licked his lips again.

Reggie rolled his eyes.

"Lick your lips."

"You wanna lick em for me?" Marcus asked.

"Ew," Reggie said.

Janie playfully pushed Reggie's arm. "Why are you so pressed? It's natural."

"Shoot, yeah," I said boldly.

"You guys are such flirts," said Janie.

I gave her "the look." It meant for her to take Reggie and get away so that me and Marcus could talk privately. But it didn't seem like she was paying attention.

No, she was downright ignoring me. We talked to Marcus and Reggie for a bit longer, then their other friends Dave and E called out to them and they had to go. When Marcus and Reggie were a safe distance away, I turned to Janie, fuming.

"Why didn't you leave when I gave you the look?" My hands were planted on my hips as I spoke.

"What are you talking about?" Janie tried to look innocent.

Yeah, right. Like she didn't know.

"Don't try to play me. You were supposed to leave so I could ask him out!" I glared at her.

"Was that what you were doing?" she asked.

I didn't like her slick tone. "Janie, I don't appreciate you trying to play me. This was not the first time you've done something like this." I was starting to heat up. "Why?"

Janie shrugged, but something was off about her demeanor. "I don't know."

I looked at her suspiciously. "You like him too, don't you?" I narrowed my eyes at her as I realized what was going on. She pretended to flirt with

Reggie while I was talking to Marcus, but the whole time, all she was really doing was blocking!

"No," she said, but her eyes betrayed her.

"You lying whore."

Janie always stole my boyfriends, had her way with them, and dumped them. I don't know why I kept forgiving her.

"Who are you calling a whore?" she said, ready for defense.

"You. What are you gonna do about it?"

"Say it again to my face!" She stepped to me.

This conversation was getting out of control. I assessed her. Janie might be a white girl, but she could definitely throw the ones. I wasn't worried, though. I was undefeated.

I stepped closer to her.

"Don't try to get gangsta on me 'cause I'll knock your old white trash self back to the trailer park!"

I knew I was out of line with that comment, but I didn't care. Janie pushed my buttons, so I had the right to push hers.

She hated being called white trash.

She swung at me, and I ducked. I pushed her to the ground. She got up and smacked me so hard I saw stars. I wasn't going down like that. I grabbed her ponytail, and then I pulled her head down to my waist and started knocking her.

She grabbed at me but missed. I knew I was being unfair by grabbing her hair, but she asked for it.

All of a sudden, someone grabbed me from behind and slammed me to the ground.

"OOOHHH!" said the crowd that had formed. I turned over and saw Midgie, the Puerto Rican girl from up the block, glaring down at me.

"Who do you think you are messing with Janie?" she said.

"I'm the girl that's about to beat you down!" I jumped up and caught Midgie with a right hook. Her ass was big, but in the heat of the moment, I felt that I could take her.

"OOOHHH!" shouted the crowd again.

Janie grabbed me by my hair and yanked me backward. I was caught off guard, so I fell. Guess that's what I got for doing the same to her. She started pounding me. Midgie was over me too, kicking me.

I tried to get up, but every time I did, Midgie kicked me down again.

Then Midgie's mother screamed for her to "bring her ass in the house," so she left with the quickness.

Then it was just me and Janie.

"COME ON, SHORTY! GET UP!" someone from the crowd yelled.

Janie sneered at me. "Let's see you try that again, trick." She started walking away, but I wasn't having that.

I leapt up from the ground, full of adrenaline. I grabbed her once again and rammed her head into my knee.

I punched her square in the face, and two front teeth fell out. She kept trying to wriggle out of my grasp, but I swung her and rammed her head through her mother's car window, setting off the alarm.

I finally stopped because I knew I had gone too far.

"Aw, shit!" I said, coming down from my rush. "Janie, are you okay?"

Janie's mother's car window was completely shattered, and there was blood coming down her forehead. I couldn't tell how bad the bleeding was, but I knew once her mom saw what I had done, it was over for me with my mom.

"Y'ALL IN TROUBLE NOW!" yelled a boy from the crowd, and everyone turned and ran when the parents started coming outside.

We lived in a huge complex with different rows of apartments connected to each other.

Just then, Janie's stance wobbled, and she fell to the ground.

Shit! I thought, my mind frantic.

"Janie, are you okay?" I repeated.

She didn't answer me.

Her mother came outside, and my mother did too. Me and Janie lived a few doors down from each other. Our moms argued with each other, and Janie's mother threatened to sue my mother to get her car window fixed, and she threatened to have me thrown in jail if Janie had any serious injuries.

After they finished arguing, my mother and I went inside our apartment, and Janie's mother swiped the glass out of her driver's seat and drove her to the hospital.

I sat on the sofa, bracing myself for what was about to come.

"Fighting!" my mother yelled. "You always fighting that girl, then y'all have the nerve to call each other friends!"

My mother was heated, for real.

I tried to fix the situation. "I'm sorry."

"You are fourteen years old, Shorty. You start high school in less than a week. You know you shouldn't be out there like this. What is your problem?"

I just looked at her. It was kind of true, what she was saying. Me and Janie had gotten into a lot of bloody fights like this one. We were always fighting. Then we always made up in a couple of days and ended up friends again. I don't know why we did it. It was just our thing.

"I know you hear me talking to you!" said my mother.

"Sorry, Ma. I don't know why we always fighting."

"Well, you're going to have to stop it!"

"I know, I know."

"I am really getting sick of you fighting that girl, and the next time you turn around, you friends! Make up your fucking minds! It's so stupid! All you do is. . . ."

She went on and on and on, ranting about how stupid I was and how I was never going to amount to anything, then my Auntie Gina came over from her apartment that was three doors down and knocked on our front door.

"Alize, who were you out there fighting?" Auntie Gina asked me. Alize is my government name, but everyone calls me Shorty.

"It wasn't that serious, Auntie!"

"Get your ass in your room!" my mother said.

I went upstairs so she and my aunt could talk about me, about how I'm always up to no good, and how I never do anything right, and blah blah blah.

The worst thing about my mother when she went on her rants was that she never felt that she had to apologize. She usually just yelled at me until she lost her voice, went to sleep, and woke up the next morning, starting all over again.

She really is a trip. All she talks about is what I do wrong.

Elida

I laid in my bed, staring at the ceiling. High school was supposed to start tomorrow, but I wasn't sure that was anything to be excited about.

I had more than a few bad experiences in middle school. Hopefully the change in scenery would come with changes in my peers' behaviors.

My name is Elida Johnson. I'm Puerto Rican and black. My eyes are gray, and my hair is black, and it goes down to my waist. I wouldn't say I'm fat, but I'm definitely thick. I have skin the color of cocoa butter.

I have no friends and no boyfriend. I've always been kind of a loner.

We live in a house that my mom rents from one of her cousins. There are no girls my age in my neighborhood. We live around a bunch of old people.

I didn't really make a lot of friends at my middle school due to everyone hating me for some reason, and now that I'm starting high school, I don't think things will get any better.

Maybe it's because I'm shy. Or maybe I give off a bad vibe or something.

I'm fourteen years old. Today happens to be my birthday.

It totally sucks that my birthday is the day before the first day of school. That's the worst time of the year to be born.

I can't walk around the school with a thrill of excitement, all of my friends showering me with gifts, people bringing me a cake and singing "Happy Birthday" to me at lunchtime, or a group of my friends jumping me for birthday hits.

I'm not saying I want people to jump me, but at least for one day, I want to feel special. For people to recognize me.

"ELIDA! You still in the freaking bed! Get the hell up. Get a freaking life, man."

My annoying little brother Sammy opened my door and walked into my room. He gets on my nerves every single day. It is pure torture living with him. He's eleven, and he's at the stage where he's always making sarcastic comments.

"What do you want?" I asked. "Leave me alone. I'm tired of you."

"Then go back to sleep," he retorted.

Little smart ass.

"Shut up. You're so annoying."

"Mommy told me to come and get you so you can clean the kitchen."

"It's not my turn."

"Well, it is now 'cause Mommy told Gabriella to do it, but she started whining, and then Mommy told her to bring her ass outside, so now she wants me to tell you to do it."

Gabriella is my little sister. She is easier to deal with than Sammy, but she is also pretty annoying too because she always tries to have whatever I have and do whatever I do. She's ten.

"Well, tell Mommy I'm still sleeping."

"No! You're woke. Go tell her your own damn self. Get up!" He turned to leave.

"Come on, man! Why can't you just tell her I'm asleep?"

"Hell no! Then she's going to try to make me do it!"

Little punk. I just stayed there in the bed, refusing to budge.

"Get up before I have to use force," he said.

"Yeah, right," I said.

"Alright, I tried to warn you."

He slapped me in the face and ran out of my room, tumbling down the stairs.

That asshole! I furiously began chasing after him. He ran into the kitchen. My mother was in there, and he ran behind her.

"Mommy!" he said. "Elida's trying to hit me 'cause I told her you said to do the kitchen!"

"No, I'm not!" I said angrily. "He came up—"

"I really don't want to hear it," said Mommy, cutting me short. "Sammy, go outside somewhere. Elida, clean this kitchen please."

She went to her room and slammed the door.

I lunged toward Sammy, but he ran out the kitchen door.

"Bastard," I mumbled bitterly. I looked around the kitchen and sighed. It was a complete mess. Dishes were all in the sink, and there were juice cans everywhere.

"Fuck my life," I said to myself. "Happy Birthday to me!" I said sarcastically, then picked up a broom.

Shorty

After me and Janie fought, I was on punishment for the next two days. I had to stay in the house. No phone or TV. Now I'm about to go to school. Hopefully Marcus will be there so I can chill with him. He's in my Biology, Algebra, and English classes. I hope he asks me out today. That boy is so fine. And he's cool and smart. Everybody wants him, but they better watch out 'cause that is MY man. Just kidding. He ain't mine. Yet.

I walked into Biology class and immediately got souped. Marcus was sitting there, and when he saw me walk in, he smiled!

"Hey, Marcus!" I said, sliding into the seat next to him. Reggie was sitting on his other side.

"Wassup, Shorty?"

"Nothing much."

"I can't get a hi?" Reggie jumped in.

I rolled my eyes in playful annoyance. "Hey, Reggie."

"Hey, is not Hi," he shot back.

I stuck out my tongue.

Marcus cut back in. "I heard you fought Janie the other day."

My ears grew kind of hot when he mentioned that he knew about my fight with Janie. I didn't know how Marcus would take something like that. I wasn't going to lie to him, but at the same time, I hoped that me getting into the fight didn't make him see me differently. *I really gotta do better.* "Yeah. I did."

"How come?" Reggie and Marcus asked in unison.

I couldn't read Marcus' expression. He looked so neutral, it was hard to tell if he looked at me differently, or not. I decided to take the safest route. Reggie just looked intrigued. "Over something stupid."

"Something stupid like what?" Marcus asked.

Dang, he was really grilling me! I didn't like to feel so off balance, like I wasn't sure what I was supposed to say, or even how I was supposed to say it, but I just hoped that Marcus wouldn't see me in a negative light after this conversation. I really needed to do better.

"She was talking junk," I tried to make my tone casual, but I don't know if it worked. I felt like my nervousness definitely had to be showing.

"Oh word? What about?"

My God, I can't take this! This boy had me too tongue tied. "I can't even remember, honestly. She was just running her mouth like she always does."

"So, yall ain't friends no more?" Reggie chimed in.

"I don't know." Just then, Janie walked into the room, rolled her eyes at me, and sat in the front with her little white girl friend, Alex.

Even though I had just spent the last five minutes sweating like a pig in heat, hoping that Marcus wasn't turned off by me now that I'd been in a fight, I did not like the look that Janie just gave me, at all. I could feel the heat rising. She was gonna learn today. "Janie!" I called out to her in a sharp tone. She turned around with attitude.

"Yeah?"

See, she always feels a need to start with me. I try my best to keep the peace, but she doesn't know how to act. "Do you have a problem?" I tried to play it cool.

She just stared a little harder, rolled her eyes, and turned back around. She whispered something into Alex's ear, then they both started giggling.

This caused me to lose what little bit of self-control I had. If this bitch wanted these hands again, she should know by now that I am all here for it. I hopped up out of my seat. I could feel everyone's eyes on me, including Marcus's.

A voice in the back of my head was telling me to just let it go, but I felt like it was too late. No way was I gonna let her punk me. As I started walking toward where Janie and Alex were sitting, Alex immediately stopped laughing, and her eyes widened in fear. *Yeah, bitch. What's so funny now?* Janie, on the other hand, was not afraid at all. Her expression was one of pure defiance. It was one of the things I loved about her, but also the reason I was about to beat that ass again.

For a moment, no one spoke, then Janie started.

"Yes?" When she opened her mouth to speak this time, I noticed that she had gotten some false teeth in place of the ones I had knocked out.

"Something funny?" I squared my shoulders.

"Yeah. You."

"Janie, don't get smart with me, or there will be even less real teeth in your mouth."

"OOOOOOOHHHH!!" our classmates exclaimed, egging our confrontation on.

"Alize," said Mr. Leslie, using my government name. I had barely realized he walked in the room, I was so heated. I knew that nothing but trouble was going to come from this, but Janie needed to learn how to stop pushing my fucking buttons.

"What?" I said to Mr. Leslie, giving him attitude.

"Go back to your seat."

"No. I want to hear what Janie got to say back."

"I said, go to your seat, right now." His tone spelled out for me that he meant business, but I ain't have time for that shit.

"And I said no."

"Shorty." I briefly snapped out of my defiant stance, hearing Marcus call my name. I turned around to face him, immediately feeling guilty. I was torn between putting Janie in her place, and keeping whatever positive image I had left in Marcus's eyes. "Come on, Ma. You don't need to get in trouble again."

His eyes pleaded with me to come back, and it turned me on, but pissed me off at the same time. Why didn't he do all that before I got up out of my seat? Now, I would just look stupid if I let it go. I briefly thought about how much trouble I would be in with my mother if I got sent home for fighting, and as much as I really, really did not want to hear her mouth, my pride got the best of me. I turned to go back to my seat, but before I started moving, I roughly pushed Janie's head.

"Don't get smart with me no more."

Now, why did I do that? I am so mean sometimes. I should have known good and well that Janie was not just going to take that. She and I had very similar personalities, which was probably why we were such close friends. She didn't back down, and I didn't back down. It was our greatest strength, while also our biggest weakness.

So, of course, Janie got up, we exchanged more words, with me becoming more and more internally embarrassed by the fact that I was probably completely destroying my chances with Marcus, but feeling completely powerless to stop myself. Before I knew it, we were fighting. Janie must have been really mad about her teeth, because for a second, she was actually winning, but then when I remembered that Marcus was watching, I mustered up every ounce of strength I had left to overtake her.

After the fight, we were both sent to the principal's office. It was neither one of our first times down this road. In the end, Janie got to go back to class because I was seen as the aggressor, and I got a three-day suspension and a phone call home to my mother.
   My mother screamed at me the entire ride home, saying she was going to kick me out of the house if I got in trouble in school one more time. I just stayed silent and looked out the window. Even though I was in deep trouble at home, the only thing I could think about was Marcus. He must really think I am a lost cause by now. I started reflecting about the whole situation from beginning to end. Why did I start that fight with Janie? She was my best friend. Once again, a voice echoed in the back of my head that I really needed to do better.

Elida

There was a fight in my Biology class. That was kind of interesting. This girl named Alize fought this other girl, Janie. At first, it seemed like Janie was winning, but then Alize must have blacked out or something because she started raining blows on her, then the teacher broke it up.

Other than that, my day was boring. I didn't make any new friends, and no guys looked at me.

The usual.

When I got home, I immediately went upstairs to my room because I felt a new poem coming to me. I rushed to get out my rhyme book before the words escaped my mind. I'm low-key something like a rapper/poet, but I think this one more closely mirrors poetry. Here it is, and don't make fun of me either:

Life

Livin in this life
It makes me wonder why

It makes me want to cry
It makes me want to DIE
I'm filled with so much pain
How can I maintain?
My heart keeps on throbbing
The me inside is sobbing
Trying to force the tears, but they won't come out
This is the worst feeling in the world
The inability to shout
The inability to cry
The anxiety in this moment
Makes me feel that all is hopeless
I just want to SCREAM!
Maybe that will set me free.

    I have notebooks and notebooks written with rhymes in them that I have never told anyone about. I would be way too embarrassed to share them with anyone, but at the same time, I keep on writing because it's my only form of release.
    "Elida!" Sammy came to my room holding the house phone in his hands.
    I almost opened my mouth to say something, but the look on his face told me it was Daddy.
    My mom and dad split up a couple years after Gabriella was born. None of us has been the same since, though my mom has been seeing a new guy off and on. She won't tell us much about him, except that they're dating. As far as I'm concerned, he can keep his ass wherever he is.
    The only man I will ever accept is my father.
    "Hello?" I answered.

"Hey Baby Girl," Daddy said.

The corners of my lips turned up. "What are you doing?"

"Nothing much. Trying to find work so I can take you guys to that new park that just opened up."

"Unique Amusements?" My heart skipped a beat.

"Yup, that's the one!"

I could hear the smile in my dad's voice. "When are we going?"

"Once I start working, I'll let you know, but it's definitely in the plans."

"Are you coming by to see us soon?"

We hadn't seen him in months.

"I sure will. Let me talk to your mother and I'll set up a date."

"Okay." I bounded out of bed and went to knock on my mother's door.

I heard her giggling on the other side. Probably talking on her cell phone with her nameless and faceless boyfriend. "What is it?" she asked.

"It's Daddy!" I made sure my voice was loud and clear in hopes that Mr. Loser would hang up the phone.

I heard Mommy suck her teeth, then she hung up with Mr. Loser.

She opened her door and took the phone from me.

I went back to my room in good spirits, then I started thinking about my life again. I want to start making friends and stuff at my new school, but I feel like I have anxiety or something, because I close up every time I try. Plus, I really don't even know who I can trust, because at previous schools, I have been kind of bullied for being the quiet, shy girl.

It's not that I'm a punk – I just don't know how to react. I have no idea why the girls didn't like me. I never did anything to them. So far, it hasn't happened yet at this school, but part of me feels like it's only a matter of time.

"Elida!" My sister, Gabriella called. *What does she want?* I sucked my teeth and sat up in my bed.

"What!" I yelled back.

"Mommy wants you!" *That fast?* What could she want me for?

I already did all my stupid chores. One of the perks of being the oldest child. You get all the responsibility, while the other kids get to go free. I sucked my teeth and slowly began to make my way back to my mother's room.

"Huh?" I said, praying that she didn't want me to do anything too exhausting.

"Close your eyes." She said. Although it was a strange request, I obeyed. This was getting interesting. I heard a rustle of paper, and my heart rate started to slightly increase. What was this about? "Okay, you can open them."

I opened my eyes to see my mother beaming at me and holding out a rectangular silver box. "Here. It's yours." I took it from her. "I didn't have no money yesterday," she continued, "but I didn't want you to think I forgot about you. Happy birthday, Elida."

I opened the box, and my jaw hit the floor. It was a silver chain with a charm on it. It said, 'Elida', and it had a diamond above the 'I'. I felt a lump form in my throat, and I blinked back tears.

I had asked my father for a chain like this for my birthday, but he said he didn't have any money. I knew my mother didn't really have it like that, so she must have sacrificed something to get this for me.

"Thank you, Mommy," I said. I really meant that, from the bottom of my heart.

"It was the least I could do," she said, her own eyes glistening with tears. "You are growing up on me. It's like I blinked, and you are in high school. I'm afraid that if I blink again, you'll be in college, living far away from me in a dorm somewhere."

I gave her a hug. When we pulled apart, she looked excited.

"Guess what?" she said.

My heart started to flutter. I felt myself getting excited too. "What?" I asked.

"That's not all you got." She pulled out two more silver boxes. One of them contained a silver bracelet that matched the pattern of the chain, and the other one had silver earrings in it. It was all so beautiful, it took my breath away. "You iced out now, girl." My mother beamed with pride.

I know I was cheesing like crazy, because this really felt like a dream. "Thank you," I managed to get out, before Gabriella barged into the room and saw all my stuff.

Her eyes widened in surprise, then anger. "That's not fair! How come she got all that? How come I ain't get none?"

"Girl, it is your big sister's birthday. When your birthday comes, you will be spoiled too. I promise."

She sucked her teeth. "You promise for real?"

"Yes, but you better remember who you call yourself sucking your teeth at. Now go back to your room and play."

She darted back toward the direction of her room. My mom chuckled. "That girl," she rolled her eyes.

"Hey, at least she will still be here when I go to college," I said.

She chuckled. "That's true. I can only imagine the arguments between her and Sammy then." My little brother and sister were always fighting.

"Stop it!" we heard, from the direction of Sammy's room.

"Hey!" my mother called out, and we heard Gabriella rushing to her room.

"Thank you," I said again.

"No problem, girl. Now get up. We are going out to eat!"

"What?" I blinked. This was all too much.

"We going to Bently's." That was a real expensive restaurant. No way she could really afford all that, plus the necklace.

"You sure?" I was reluctant to go. I definitely wanted to, but I didn't want to put my mother out either.

"Girl, it is your birthday. Get dressed."

Shorty

When I finally got back to school after my suspension, I decided that it was time for a change. I wasn't going to fight anymore with Janie, or anyone else, for that matter. I wasn't going to chase after Marcus so much anymore either. And this time, I was actually going to submit my make-up work. I walked into class, feeling all new and shiny. Well, maybe not new and shiny, but definitely different. I sat down in my spot next to Marcus.

"Wassup, Shorty? You good?"

Reggie looked over at me too.

My heart fluttered slightly at the fact that Marcus cared how I was doing, but at the same time, I wanted to keep my focus. I didn't want to break this promise that I made to myself. "Nothing much. Just trying to get back on track. What's up with you?"

"It's been so boring in science class without you," he said. Once again, my heart fluttered. I felt like I had to get a grip, or I was going to lose this battle, fast.

I smiled at him. "Really?"

"Yeah, girl. You're mad cool."

OMG! Was he playing with me? My little promise about leaving him alone was swiftly flying toward the window. He couldn't be talking to me like this and expect me to retain my composure.

Just then, this girl named Elida walked in. She had on this really nice chain with her name on it.

"Hey, girl!" I said. I didn't know why I was being so friendly all of a sudden. Maybe it was because I was trying to turn over a new leaf. Or maybe I was just trying to distract myself from Marcus, with his deep, dark chocolate skin, perfect fade, and juicy lips. The struggle was real.

Elida turned toward me, looking kind of surprised. At that moment, my heart panged. I had a flashback of the first day or two of class. She pretty much kept to herself. No one talked to her, and she talked to no one. *I wonder if she has any friends?*

"Hey," she said, looking kind of awkward, like she didn't know how to take me.

"That is a really dope chain, girl," I said, trying to let her know that I wasn't coming at her with bad intentions. "Is that real? Where did you get it?"

She blushed. "My mom got it for me. For my birthday."

"Oh, it's your birthday? Happy birthday, girl!"

"Thanks. It was last week."

She stood there for a few moments as if she wasn't sure how to proceed, so I decided to make it easy for her. "Why don't you come sit with us? You don't have to sit all the way over there by yourself." I gestured toward the seat next to me. Elida sat down. She and Marcus were on either side of me now.

The teacher walked in and was ready to start the lesson. We spent the period passing notes back and forth between me, Elida, Marcus, and Reggie. It was so much fun.

Elida seemed kind of quiet, but that might be just the kind of friend I need.

I saw Janie shooting a couple of glances toward us throughout the period, probably wondering why I started talking to Elida, but it was really none of her business. Okay, maybe that was harsh, especially since she was my best friend, but I could have other friends too, right?

At my next class, Janie immediately came over and sat next to me.

"What do you want?" I asked, still kind of upset about our fight.

"Look, Shorty. I'm sorry about what happened."

"Yeah, me too," I admitted.

"How are things with Marcus?"

"The same." I rolled my eyes. "He is so fine, but he needs to stop playing with my emotions."

Her eyes lit up. "Playing with your emotions how?" Her eyebrow raised.

"Girrrl, let me tell you!" I went on to spill the beans about how Marcus may have potentially been flirting with me the last couple of classes. I was super lit.

"Wow. You guys would be so cute together," said Janie.

"I know. He needs to stop playing and just say something."

"Right," she agreed, but then her expression changed slightly. "So anyway, why were you talking to that girl?"

"Who, Elida?"

"Yeah."

"I don't know. I was tired of seeing her by herself all the time. She seems like a nice girl."

"I don't think you should start hanging with her."

"Why not?"

"Because! Didn't you see the way Marcus was eyeing her?" My heart dropped.

"Marcus was not eyeing her."

"Shorty. He totally was."

"Are you sure?"

"Definitely."

This revelation made me want to reconsider my new friendship with Elida. I truly hoped that Janie didn't know what she was talking about, because I have been crushing on Marcus for as long as I can remember, and it seems like we are so close to actually being official. I tried to remain optimistic.

"I mean, she is a pretty girl. Just because he may have looked at her doesn't mean he wants to be with her."

"But what if he does?"

"Then that's not her fault. Besides, she probably has a boyfriend anyway."

Janie snorted. "That loser? Yeah, right. She probably has never even touched a boy before."

"That's really messed up, Janie. Why are you talking about her like that?"

"Because I don't like her."

"How do you not like her when you don't even know her?"

"I don't know. I just don't."

"How do you not know?"

"Maybe it's because she has no friends. No one else likes her."

"I doubt that's true. But even if it was, do you have to be like everybody else?"

"I'm not like everybody else. I just don't like the bitch."

"You're mean."

"Why are you getting all defensive about her anyway?"

"She seems pretty cool to me."

"You don't even know her."

"Neither do you."

"Whatever." She sucked her teeth. "Just don't expect me to start hanging with her too."

Elida

Well, today wasn't as predictable as the others. I might have actually made a friend. Alize seems kind of cool. Marcus and Reggie too. But Marcus kept, like, staring at me over Alize's shoulder. I never had a boy look at me like that before. Boys never look at me.

It probably didn't mean anything anyway. He probably thinks I'm hideous. I wouldn't be surprised at that.

Yet I had a dream about him last night. I know, I'm a total weirdo, but in the dream, Marcus was my boyfriend, and he actually kissed me! Isn't that crazy? But what sucked was that as soon as he kissed me, the dream ended. I was so mad! I wanted to see what would happen next!

As stalkerish as it sounds, I actually wrote a poem about him. Well, not really about him, but about guys in general. Here it is:

The Wish

    I wish for you to wish for me
    You be the one that sets me free
    Love me and like me to your own accord
    I don't want to have forced you
    -     No past casting of spells
    When I look in your eyes, I'll be able to tell
    Whether there should be wedding or warning bells
    To feel your tongue slide in my mouth
    To hear you talk without feeling left out
    To have you hold me and recite your dreams
    To see you with me – It's more intense than it seems
    I wish to walk with you and hold your hand
    I want you to KISS me – and not by demand
    Your chocolate body, and skin so smooth
    Like I said before, I got a sweet tooth
    This is the way I wish life was for me
    -     Which I know will NEVER be REALITY
    -     And FOREVER a DREAM.

    I know, I know, my poems are terrible. But I have to let all these thoughts and feelings out somehow. It's therapeutic. I think I might be depressed. Sometimes I feel like I will never be happy. Like it's just not in the cards for me. I basically just sit here and stare at the ceiling and dream all these dreams, and write all these poems that I share with no one.
    I don't know what else to do though. The Pastor at church always talks about how you can

tell God all your problems, but what if He doesn't even listen? What if He doesn't respond? If even God doesn't understand me, who else could I possibly turn to? I don't know. Maybe I shouldn't even be thinking this way.

Honestly, the way my life is set up, I don't know how else to think.

Shorty

I was walking through the mall with Janie when I spotted a group of rowdy looking females coming toward us. There were about five of them. I quickly picked out who their leader was. She was the maddest looking one. It was this girl named Shaneeda Jackson. She abruptly stopped in front of me. I geared myself up for a random confrontation.

"I heard you was sleeping with my man, bitch." She crossed her arms over her chest and gave me a nasty stare.

Oh God. I really didn't have time for this. I had been doing so good lately with turning over my new leaf, but here comes this crazy bitch about to test my patience! Bitches should know by now that I don't give a fuck! I could feel myself getting hot. I tried to calm down, but my temper was rising.

"Shaneeda. What are you talking about?" My response was short and to the point. I prayed that she would just walk away and leave me alone, but you never knew with dusty bitches like this.

"You heard me. I don't need to repeat myself."

"Look, I don't have a problem with you, and I don't even know your nasty ass man. No, I haven't been sleeping with him, whoever he is."

"What makes you think I'm supposed to believe that, just because you said it? Bitch, I have the receipts!"

My insides were boiling by now. I was starting to lose control. "What receipts? You can't possibly have receipts, because I don't know your man!"

"Let's take this outside." She started walking toward the exit. I followed. I ain't scared of shit. These bitches might jump me, but Janie got my back. They may win, but not without a fight. We went over to the side of the mall, where there were no security guards.

"Imma let you know, right here and right now, Shorty, that I never liked you. And now I find out you are sleeping with my man?"

"Like I told you before, and I'm telling you again now, I never slept with your man, and I don't even know him."

"Bitch, stop lying!" She grabbed out her phone and scrolled until she found some screenshots. "He didn't even bother to fucking change your name!"

I looked at the phone and saw a whole bunch of messages between her man and a girl named Shorty. It damn sure wasn't me, but from the couple of messages I read, they definitely slept together.

"That's not me. I don't know who your man even is." I looked to my side to check Janie, but she wasn't next to me.

My head whipped around, trying to figure out where she was. I was so caught up in anger that I never realized she didn't follow us out of the mall. So now I was left alone with a pack of five angry bitches, and my so-called best friend is nowhere to be found.

"Look, bitch, this is undeniable truth." She put her phone back in her pocket and started rolling her hair up. I squared up myself, trying to keep eyes on all five of them at once. This was definitely about to be some bullshit.

Shaneeda swung at me, but I could tell she was scared. The only reason she probably even confronted me in the first place was because her friends were there. I easily grabbed her hand and twisted that bitch, kicking her legs out from underneath her to get her on the ground.

As I proceeded to beat her ass, her friends grabbed me off of her and got me on the ground. They started kicking and hitting me. I fought back as hard as I could. I hit a few of them, but I'm not a fucking superhero – I can't take five bitches on my own.

I tried my best to cover my face, because these were those scratching type bitches, but one of them got me. I just hoped it wouldn't look too bad and that it would heal quickly. While we were in the middle of all this commotion, the security guards must have spotted us, because I heard someone yell, "FREEZE!"

The next thing I knew, Shaneeda and her friends were scattering in five different directions, and I was laying on the ground by myself.

Two security guards quickly approached me. "Ma'am, are you okay?"

"I just got jumped. What the fuck do you think?" I knew it was uncalled for, but I was heated. My best friend just bounced on me and let all these bitches jump me. I stood up, and I started to wobble a little. The other guard reached out to steady me.

"We should get you to the hospital."

At the hospital, the doctors cleaned me up. Shaneeda and her friends didn't get me too bad. I had a black eye, and my side hurt a lot from all that kicking, but besides that, I just had a little scratch on my face from where the girl got me. My mother was in worse shape than I was. When we finally got home, she was yelling and screaming at the top of her lungs.

"What the hell is your problem? Why are you always fighting? Who was it this time, Shorty? And for what stupid reason? You need to stop messing around like this, or you're either going to end up dead, or in jail just like your fucking father! I don't know why I still put up with your stupid ass! I should just send you off somewhere and let social services take over. Why can't you do anything right? Got me getting up out my bed at 11 o'clock at night because you want to fight somebody and got your ass whooped. What the hell is wrong with you?"

This went on for over an hour, until she was exhausted and her voice gave out. Once that happened, she sent me to bed.

I went upstairs and cried for a long time. Why was my mother so mean to me? I mean, I understand she was mad at me for fighting, but did she have to say all that? She never even asked if I was okay. She didn't even know that I wasn't the one who initiated the fight. Her words kept running through my mind over and over again: *"I don't know why I still put up with your stupid ass!"* My mind went to my father. He was serving the last four years of a ten-year sentence for armed robbery and assault.

I missed him so much, but we didn't get to see each other due to him being over two hours away and my mother not wanting to bring me.

We kept up over the phone, but it wasn't the same.

My mind went back to my mother. Those girls could have put me in a coma or something, and I bet she would still blame it on me. Like I went up to them and asked them to jump me or something.

It seems like things just keep coming at me for no reason. I really am trying to do better, but no matter what I do, it's not good enough. I went to sleep that night, praying, "God. Please just make me better. Please make me better so my mother will love me. I'll do anything. Please just help me."

Elida

I walked into science class feeling confident. I don't know why; I just felt that way. Then I noticed that something was wrong. Alize was sitting down looking pissed off. She had a black eye. I immediately got angry. *Who did this to her?*

I walked over to where she, Marcus, and Reggie were sitting.

"Alize, what happened?" I asked, concerned.

"I got jumped."

As soon as I heard those words, my anger rose higher. I had a flashback of all the times I was bullied, and people used to hit me and do all types of evil shit. There was no way I was letting this happen to her, too. "By who? When?"

She looked up at me in surprise. She was probably wondering why I even cared that much, I sort of wondered why, too, but all I knew was that whoever did this was not getting away with it.

"This girl named Shaneeda, and four of her friends."

"Why did they jump you?"

"Supposedly, she thought I was sleeping with her man, but even when I told her that I didn't even know her fucking man, she didn't believe me. She showed me some screenshots of him talking to some girl named Shorty, then they jumped me."

"That's some punk shit! So they just came and jumped you when they didn't even know for sure it was you?"

"I guess she figured that since I'm the only girl named Shorty in this school, it had to be me."

"And why couldn't she just fight you one on one, if she really believed it was you?"

"That's how scary bitches do. But Imma get that bitch though. Believe that."

"Make sure you bring me with you." I surprised both myself and Shorty with those words. "I got your back." I didn't know where all this boldness was coming from, but I liked it.

"You serious?" Shorty said, looking shocked.

"Yeah." She smiled, and I smiled back. I sat down next to her, and we started talking about other stuff.

I probably sound really crazy making promises to help Shorty get Shaneeda back, but I really just cannot stand any form of bullying. It happened to me, and no one was there to help. Thankfully, all those girls went to different high schools, but I was never letting that happen again. Not to me, and definitely not to Shorty. I don't really know her that well yet, but my intuition tells me that she is a good person.

I feel like we just click.

Shorty

I went to the bathroom during lunch, and Janie was in there, sitting on the floor against the wall. I was kind of shocked when I saw her. She had ignored all my calls and texts that I sent her, demanding to know why she left me to get jumped, and today, I thought she didn't show up to school because she wasn't in the first two classes we had together. Now I find out she has been hiding in the bathroom all day. *What the hell is wrong with this girl?*

She looked up when she saw me. "Oh, what's up?"

"What's up? That's all you have to say after what you did to me? Where the fuck were you, Janie? I took my eyes off you for one second, and when I looked back, you were gone!" I wanted to drag her, right here in this bathroom, but first I needed to know what the hell was going on.

"What are you talking about?"

"Don't play with me, Janie. Shaneeda and all her friends jumped me. Why didn't you help me?"

"I tried. I went to get the security guards, but I couldn't find you. I..."

"BULLSHIT!" I shouted. "You knew damn well where I was. That's where everybody fights, Janie. You just chose not to follow."

"I'm sorry."

"And where the hell did Shaneeda get the idea that I was with her man? I don't even know that dumb broad like that."

"I don't know."

"Well you and her talk sometimes. Shouldn't you know?" She looked at me, and her eyes shifted. There was something she wasn't telling me. "What is it, Janie?"

"Nothing."

"What the hell is it?"

"Um... someone has been sleeping with her man."

"Okay, that's already been established. But what the hell does that have to do with me? Why didn't you tell her who it actually was, so she could jump that person?"

"I couldn't tell her."

"What do you mean, you couldn't tell her? You sure as hell didn't have a problem with letting her think I did it. Who was it?" She just stared at me. "Probably one of those lame ass bitches that helped her jump me."

"No..." her voice trailed off.

"Who, then? You?" I joked. I was tired of this guessing game.

Janie looked down.

Hold up! I know she just didn't... "You were the one sleeping with her man?"

"Yeah."

I quickly put two and two together. "So you mean to tell me that you catfished this nigga using my name, and didn't bother telling me about it? Then you let me get caught off guard at the mall?"

"I didn't know she was going to do all that."

"Of course if she found out her man was cheating, she was gonna want to fight, Janie! You know that shit! How could you betray me like this? This is snake shit!"

"I'm sorry. I couldn't tell her, because I knew she would want to fight me, and I can't fight anyone right now. I'm pregnant."

I had already opened my mouth to continue cussing Janie out, but those words made me pause. "You're telling me that you are pregnant with Shaneeda's man's baby?"

She nodded. "That's why I couldn't tell her."

"How long have you known this? Are you gonna keep it? Did you tell Shaneeda's man? Janie, what the fuck! Why are you not wearing protection?"

"It feels better without it."

I was speechless. This situation was too much for me. I didn't know what to think about Janie. I didn't know whether she was a snake that just got me jumped, or just someone who got caught up in some BS and didn't know what else to do. I shook my head.

"Wow, Janie. Wow."

I left the bathroom so I could get to my next class before the final bell rang.

Elida

I remember the first time I experienced bullying.

I was in sixth grade, and we were in the locker room getting changed for gym class. This girl named Glenda walked up to me, claiming that I was a "copycat bitch" for having my hair braided in a similar style to hers.

"What are you talking about? I never even saw your hair before I got mine done!"

Of course, Glenda and her friends didn't believe me, so they started taunting me. By the time the gym class started, some of the boys were in on it too.

From that day forward, the bullying continued and only got worse, with Glenda and her friends smearing stuff on my locker, tripping me in the hallways, and threatening to jump me when the teachers weren't around.

I told my mom what was going on, and she went up to the school for a conference.

After that, I was labeled a snitch and the bullying only got worse.

In seventh grade, I went to a new school.

I thought I was finally free, until I realized that one of Glenda's best friends Zaida also transferred to the new school, and the bullying continued.

I didn't bother to tell my mom about what was happening to me this time.

I just held it in and kept to myself to the best of my ability. My notebooks were filled with poems that described my experiences. It was the only way I could cope.

By the stroke of a miracle, I scored three friends my first week of high school. Things seem to be turning around for me.

I wonder what it feels like to be kissed. To have somebody's lips on mine. I wonder if it's really as magical as they make it look in movies, and how they describe it in books. I wonder if it will ever happen for me...

I'm tired of being embarrassed whenever I hear groups of girls talking about their boyfriends, or their experiences with boys. If anyone ever asked me, I would have nothing to share. My only stories that have to do with boys involve me being severely rejected. I wrote a poem about this a while back:

You Feel Me?

I want to know what it's like
To feel real, to be exposed
To a happy reality, to the kind of life I would have chose

I question why? But no one seems to know
I'm pushing forward, holding back
Want it to stay a mystery, yet be unfolded
Why do I think like this?
Why me? What's the problem?
Am I the only one, or are other's hearts being robbed from them?
Do you FEEL ME? Do you UNDERSTAND what I'm saying?
Or are you just sitting there
For the end of this poem, PATIENTLY WAITING?

You're probably thinking, *this bitch has a poem for everything.* But as I said before, it's the only way I have to let it out. Maybe I need to get my head checked or something.

Shorty

I walked into my house after school, feeling completely exhausted. This was a long ass day. I walked into the kitchen and got the shock of my life. My mom was sitting at the table, crying. Her hair was all messed up. She had a beer bottle in her hand. She looked straight hit up.

"Ma, what's wrong?" I immediately felt for her.

"Ronald dumped me." Ronald is, well, was her boyfriend. They had been going out for almost a year. To be honest, I'm happy they broke up. I hated the guy. He was mad fake and annoying. He always thinks he knows everything, and he low-key was always trying to make passes at me. But enough of that. Back to my mother.

"Are you going to be okay?" I didn't like to see her like this. She looked so sad. I felt a surge of hatred for Ronald. She shook her head at me. "What?" I asked.

"I can't believe he left me."

I walked over to her. "It's gonna be okay, Ma. Don't worry about it." I put my arms around her to hug her, but she pushed me so hard that I hit my back on the corner of the counter and knocked over a beer bottle on the way to the floor. My body was filled with instant pain. My back felt a very sharp pang from the counter, and I cut my arm on the beer bottle that I accidentally knocked over. There was beer all over my clothes. I stared up at her in shock. She stood over me, her expression filled with hatred.

"THIS IS ALL YOUR FUCKING FAULT!" I stared at her.

"What?"

"He left me because of you. He told me that he was tired of you always getting an attitude with him, and how you never listen to anything he says!" I stared at her. My hatred for Ronald grew. I had never been rude to the guy. Even when he tried to get with me, I let him down as respectfully as possible. I didn't know what he was talking about.

"I was never rude to him." I slowly rose to my feet, my arm stinging. Pain was shooting through my back as well. I need to get some ice or something.

"Yes, you were! He told me! I know you're lying, Shorty."

"Ma, stop yelling. Sit down. You're having a bad day, that's all." I tried to direct her to her seat, but she pushed me back and smacked my face. It burned. My eyes filled with tears, as my heart filled with hurt.

"Don't you touch me! Ain't nothing but bad coming from you! Nothing but bad, and I don't need no more!"

How could she say something like that to me? I'm standing here, bleeding and in pain, and she is basically talking like she hates me? I looked down at my arm. It wasn't cut deeply, but it did sting, and the blood was starting to drip to the floor. I made my way over to the sink to wash it and get a paper towel to stop the blood before I found a band aid.

"You're replacing that beer, too. Don't think you ain't."

"What?"

"You dropped it, so you're gonna pay for it."

"It wasn't my fault!"

"I don't give a fuck! You shouldn't have touched me!"

"Ma..."

"You always ruining something. Don't you have anything good about you? You fight. You do bad in school. Your grades are horrible... What do you even have? Nothing!"

"I'm trying to bring my grades up."

"Bullshit."

"I am."

"Ronald told me he tried to help you with your homework, and you told him you didn't need any help."

"Ma, that never happened."

She rolled her eyes like she didn't believe me. "Just get the fuck out of here."

What was wrong with my mother? I stood there, fighting back tears.

"What? You going to cry now? Don't be mad at me for telling you the truth."

I blocked out the rest of my mother's words as I slowly cleaned and bandaged my cut, swept and mopped the glass and beer from the floor, and went up to my room to be by myself.

Elida

I walked into science class and sat next to Marcus. Shorty walked in a little after me and pulled up a chair on the other side of us. Reggie came in after us and gave Shorty a strange glance before he sat on my other side.

Shorty looked like she had been through hell and back. Or maybe like she was still there. Reggie was the first one to speak.

"What's wrong with you, Ma?"

She just looked at him and shook her head.

"Are you going to be okay?" I asked.

She shrugged. "I don't think so."

"What happened?" asked Marcus.

"Nothing. I'm just... going through some things."

"What kind of things?" Reggie asked. "You look like you are spaced out. Come on, Shorty. This ain't like you."

I was thinking the same thing.

We stared at her, waiting for an explanation.

"I don't want to talk about it."

Marcus sighed. "Well… alright then. Let us know when you're ready."

"Okay." She said, and stared blankly into space.

Marcus and I exchanged looks.

Reggie just kept staring at Shorty.

Something was seriously wrong with her. I hoped that it wasn't anything too bad. Whatever it was, though, we would definitely be there for her.

The teacher walked in and was ready to begin the lesson. Today we were doing a bunch of experiments at different stations around the classroom. We had to travel from space to space and write up a little report as we went through them all. Of course, Marcus, Shorty, Reggie, and I chose to work together as a group, but it was more so the rest of us that were doing the work. Shorty was completely out of it, but it was clear that she was not feeling well, so it was no problem.

Shorty's other friend, Janie, kept staring over at us. She looked like she was trying to see what was up with Shorty, but then she also kept shooting me little dirty looks.

I don't know where that is coming from. I have never spoken to Janie in my life. The only way I even know her name is because the teacher says it when he takes attendance, and because she is Shorty's friend.

I wonder what's up with that?

Marcus

Me and Reggie headed to the locker room to get set up for gym. We shared the same class with our boys Dave and E.

"Yo, what you think is up with Shorty?" Reggie asked.

He took the words right out of my mouth.

"No idea, bro. I just hope she's okay."

"Right."

Dave and E walked in the locker room with some other guys.

"Ready to get that ass busted?" E said, looking at me when he spoke.

I felt myself growing hot as my competitive spirit rose within me. "We'll see whose ass is busted by the end of the game."

We changed and went out into the gym, where we saw that we had a substitute.

Instead of letting us continue our mini basketball tournaments, she forced us to play

Bocce instead. Of course, me and my boys was pissed off, but we kept our cool.

We would just have to wait for Mr. Rivers to come back.

"I'm thinking of trying out for the team next year," Reggie blurted out while the teacher was separating us.

"The basketball team?" I asked.

"Duh," E cut in.

"I was thinking of joining too," Dave said.

"Damn, maybe we should all try out."

"Why not this year?" E asked. "They starting tryouts in a couple of days."

I immediately grew nervous. Not that I couldn't play, but I knew street ball was a lot different from organized sports.

Dave chimed in. "You don't think we should do more practice first?"

E shook his head. "What need would we have? We been playing basketball since we learned how to dribble!"

"I think we should watch the tryouts, but not necessarily join."

E looked at me like I was stupid. "What kind of shit is that? Why the hell would you watch, but not play?"

I opened my mouth to say something, but the teacher was pointing at me. "Young man, I want you to go on the green team."

She had separated us into four colored teams: green, yellow, black, and blue.

Of course, our whole crew was separated so we didn't get to talk much during the rest of the class period.

By the time gym class was over, we had to rush back to the locker rooms to change because the teacher mixed up the time schedule.

I was low key relieved because I was sick of E's shit-talking anyway.

Shorty

I walked into the bathroom, went against the wall, and slid to the floor. I just wanted to go the hell home. This was not a good day. All I could think about was my mother's harsh words from the day before. Little flashbacks kept coming back to my mind. *This is all your fuckin fault! Nothing but bad is ever coming from you...*

I couldn't believe she said all that stuff to me. It's like she gave up on me or something. Even when I told her I was trying to do better, she laughed in my face. Like it wasn't even a possibility that I was trying.

All of a sudden, the bathroom door banged open, and Shaneeda and one of her friends walked in. Just my fucking day. She saw me and smirked.

"Bitch."

"Don't start with me today, Shaneeda. I ain't the one."

"What you gonna do? Get your ass whooped again?"

"You didn't whoop my ass. You jumped me. And if I remember correctly, it was you getting your ass whooped when your punk ass friends jumped in."

"Who you calling a punk?" The other girl said, stepping around Shaneeda.

"You, bitch!" I stood up.

"You don't want it with me, trust."

"You ain't beating my ass, so I ain't worried."

"Well, let's see about that." She started wrapping up her hair and kicking off her heels. Of course, Shaneeda started doing the same. I rolled my eyes. These scary bitches was really about to jump me again.

The bathroom door banged open. "What's going on here?"

All of our heads whipped toward the direction of the voice. It was Elida. *Yass! Come through, bihh!* I thought.

"These punk bitches trying to jump me again," I said.

"Oh, so you're Shaneeda?" Elida said, walking in our direction. Immediately, both Shaneeda and her friend started to back away. I shook my head in disgust.

"Yes, and?" said Shaneeda, still trying to retain her attitude, but everyone could tell she was scared now that it was actually a fair fight.

"I'm only going to say this once," said Elida. "Nobody is going to jump Shorty. Not on my watch. If you want it with her, you want it with me too."

Shaneeda started putting her heels back on. Her friend started doing the same. "Come on, Shakeeka," she said, and they turned toward the door.

At the revelation of Shaneeda's friend's name, Elida and I turned toward each other, then burst out laughing at the same time.

Shakeeka looked embarrassed. "Ain't shit funny, bitch!" She and Shaneeda exited the bathroom.

I sighed in relief. "Thank God that's over."

"But Shakeeka though?" said Elida, raising her eyebrows.

"Girl, stop!" I tried not to laugh again. "My momma named me Alize, so I can't really talk."

"Hey, what was going on with you earlier?" Elida's expression switched to concern.

"I just been going through some things with my mother." My mood immediately sobered.

"Like what?"

At first, I was going to brush her off, but she looked so sincere, I felt like I could trust her. Also, she had literally just stood up for me, risked getting suspended and everything, when she barely even knew me, so I let loose. I told her everything that was going on with my mother. When I finished, I felt much better. We spent the rest of the day skipping class in various bathrooms throughout the school. You had to be slick about it, because teachers checked before each class.

Elida is so cool. It's like we immediately clicked. But one thing about her is that she seemed kind of distant. *I wonder what that's all about?*

Whatever it is, I just want to help her, like she helped me.

Elida

I really made a friend. Shorty is so cool. I hope the teachers don't call home or anything saying that they didn't see us in class. I've never skipped any class before. I was kind of scared throughout the day, thinking that we would get caught, but Shorty was a pro.

I am so glad that I walked into that bathroom at just the right time. Shorty was right – those girls were punks. They were all set and ready to jump her when they thought she was alone, but then when I came, they immediately backed down.

I felt good to be there for Shorty, when nobody was there for me. I have so many memories of girls hitting me, pulling my hair, and saying all kinds of mean things about me. No one came to my rescue. No one. If just one person had stepped up, maybe I wouldn't have had to suffer the way I did. Maybe I wouldn't spend most of my days afraid to talk to people and staring at the ceiling. Maybe I wouldn't have all of those notebooks full of dark and depressing poems. Maybe my life would be different.

Daddy was supposed to take us to Unique Amusements today. Sammy and Gabriella were so excited about it. I was kind of excited too, but at the same time, nervous.

I tried to call Daddy the other day, and he usually picked up, but this time he didn't. I tried not to think of what that probably meant, but I couldn't help it. Last time it happened, Daddy cancelled on us. And the time before that.

No sooner than the thought entered my mind, I heard Sammy's room door slam.

"Hey!" Mommy called out in a sharp tone.

"Leave me alone!" he said, but his voice sounded like a strangled grunt rather than an attitude.

My heart sank.

I got up and opened my door, stepping into the hallway. Mommy was staring at Sammy's door like she wanted to say something. I looked in Gabriella's room, and she was sitting there quiet, playing on her tablet. She was too quiet though. Usually she acted excited or giggled or something.

I opened my mouth to ask Mommy what was wrong, when she looked at me with a pained expression. "Your father said he couldn't make it."

Then I understood why my siblings were upset.

I was hurt too, because this wasn't the first time it happened. It seemed like it happened more often than not. I blinked back my emotions.

"It's okay, Mommy."

She moved to say something, but decided against it. Her facial expression changed. "You know what?" she said, getting a smile on her face. "Sammy! Gabriella! How about we go to the movies!"

Gabriella looked up from her tablet. Sammy didn't say anything from his room.

Mommy opened his door, and he was lying on his bed.

"Sammy, do you want to go?" Mommy asked.

"I guess," he responded.

We went and had a great time. At first, Sammy was still feeling down and out, but he lightened up when Mommy let him pick the second movie. Gabriella had picked the first one.

Marcus

E talked a lot of shit in gym class, but I could tell he was nervous too. We all signed up for the junior varsity tryouts. We went on YouTube and practiced the day before, and E was confident that he would make the varsity team.

I had to admit, he was pretty good. I was hoping I at least made junior varsity.

Mr. Rivers was not only our gym teacher; he was also the basketball coach. Now that I think of it, that's probably why he let us do the mini basketball tournaments the first couple of days of class. He was probably trying to scout out the good players.

"Fellas!" he said, when we walked in the gym. "Somehow I knew I would see you four."

There were a bunch of other kids from our grade there too, along with sophomores. Coach Rivers also had the varsity players sitting on the bleachers. I couldn't tell if they were there to watch or intimidate us. Maybe both.

We started doing drills, and I found that it wasn't too difficult.

"Okay guys!" Coach Rivers said after we finished full court dribbles. "Now, we're going to try some form shooting."

He called one of the varsity players, an upperclassman named Rex, up to the plate. "Rex, I want you to demonstrate these shots."

Rex smirked and proceeded to show off, effortlessly doing each shot Coach Rivers told him to do. That made me nervous as hell, but I studied him as he moved, praying I could execute them.

Coach had us going one by one, and he called me first.

"Marcus! You're up!"

Rex threw me the ball, and thankfully I caught it with ease. I dribbled a few seconds before I took my first shot. I missed.

"Come on, nigga!" said E.

"Hey!" Coach Rivers barked. "I understand you're trying to encourage your friend, but clean up the language."

E got quiet after that.

"Try again," Coach said, and passed me the ball.

I shot four more shots from different angles and made them all.

Coach called another kid next, and the tryout continued.

By the end of it, all of us were more tired from nerves than anything.

"Damn, how you think you did?" Reggie asked me.

We were walking home.

Before I could answer, E cut in. "I know I definitely made varsity. You too, Reggie. I'm not sure about these niggas though," he chuckled, gesturing toward me and Dave.

"Fuck you," me and Dave said.

In my opinion, E didn't do as well as he thought he did. He had trouble following the coaches' directions even though he made most of his shots.

Reggie was a natural. He looked like he was made for the team. Dave did pretty much the same as I did, with missing his first shot when we did the form drills, but making the others.

We had two more days of tryouts, then Coach Rivers was posting the kids who made it on Friday. I was sweating bullets.

Reggie

In my opinion, somebody needs to check that nigga E, but I'm not gonna speak on it though. After the first day of tryouts, his shit talking kept getting worse.

Then when Coach posted the final team members on Friday, his ass was pissed he didn't make it.

I was glad it was the end of the school day, because now those who didn't make the team didn't have to walk around all day with sad faces.

I made varsity, which was a surprise, and Marcus and Dave made junior varsity. It was awkward to have everybody on the team except E, but we tried to make him feel better.

"Whatever niggas, that team ain't shit anyway," he said. "I'll catch y'all later."

He started walking off, and of course we followed him.

"You can try out next year," Dave offered.

E didn't say anything.

He just started aggressively approaching this other freshman from a different school as he went down a side street. The kid was wearing brand new Jordan's, and had another pair slung over his shoulders, connected by their laces.

His head was in his phone, so he wasn't paying attention while he was walking.

E was a lot bigger than the kid, so when he approached him, the kid stopped short, startled.

The kid pulled his earbud from his left ear. "What's up, man?" He stared at E, then glanced at us and took a step back.

"What size are those Jordan's?" E asked.

The kid looked nervous.

It finally dawned on me what E was doing. Dave jumped in. "Look like your size, E."

My eyes shot to Marcus.

We had never robbed anybody before, so E's behavior came as a surprise. I could tell Dave was just trying to make E feel better for not making the team, but still, this kid had nothing to do with that.

"E," Marcus said.

"Shut the fuck up, nigga! Don't be spreading my government."

E snatched the kid's sneakers off his shoulders.

"Hey man, give those back!" the kid said, but I could tell he was scared. There were four of us, and one of him.

"Come on, E," I said.

"Nah, this nigga walking around advertising his shit. Since he got so many pairs, he won't miss these too much."

E slid his own sneakers off his feet, disconnected the laces from the new Jordan's, and put them on. "You right, Dave. Just my size."

"Those are mine!" the kid said.

E just mocked him.

I could tell Dave felt bad because the kid looked like he was about to cry, but he went along with E. "Shouldn't have let nobody catch you slipping."

I couldn't even look the kid in his eyes as we all continued walking down the street. I glanced back when we were turning a corner and saw him still standing there, looking lost.

Shorty

It's report card day. This is our first one of freshman year. I have been working as hard as I could to remain true to my promise, not getting into any more fights since the time I got jumped, and actually paying attention in class and doing my homework.

Maybe now I can finally show my mother all my progress, and I will have proof. I just hope my grades are good. I will be devastated if they aren't.

The whole day, as last period approached, my heart rate slightly increased, and I became more and more nervous. I even started to sweat a little during the last two periods. I know it's only the first marking period, but if you had the home life I did, you would understand.

After our last class, we were all sent to our homerooms to finally get our report cards. Elida, Marcus, Reggie, and I were all in the same homeroom. I was shaking like crazy.

"Chill, Shorty," Marcus said, trying to get me to relax.

"It's not that serious. You will do fine." Elida smiled.

"What if it's horrible? She will hate me!" By this time, I had also filled Marcus and Reggie in on everything that went on with my mother. Marcus was furious to find out, and threatened to call the police or CPS, but I told him I was fine.

"You are more important than your grades," said Reggie, and I really felt his words. I swallowed back a lump in my throat.

"Alize Henderson." The teacher said, calling me up to the front to receive my grades. We had been so engrossed in our conversation, we hadn't noticed that the teacher had already started calling people. I slowly got up and made my way to the front of the room.

"Knock em dead, kid," said Mrs. Robinson, our teacher, with a smile. She looked at me like she knew my situation or something. I wanted to say something to her, but she was busy calling all of our names, so I just said, "Thank you,", signed my name to confirm receiving the report, and scurried back to my seat.

"What did she say to you?" Elida whispered.

"She was encouraging me." I blushed.

"Unfold it!" said Marcus. He looked more nervous than I felt.

"Elida Johnson," said Mrs. Robinson. Elida got up and went to get her report card. When she came back, she looked at the paper in my hand that was still folded.

"Do not tell me you still haven't looked!" she chided.

"I was waiting for you," I said, trying to play it off.

"Come on, Shorty," said Reggie. "Shoot, you got me nervous over here."

"Could you do it for me?" I asked Marcus.

He raised his eyebrows. "Okay," he reached for it, but then Mrs. Robinson called his name.

"Marcus Stanton."

"Hold on, Ma. I'll be right back." He walked up to where the teacher was, signed for his report card, then came back.

Elida was looking at hers.

"What did you get?" I said, my anxiety at an all time high.

"Four A's, three B's."

"Okay, okay! Get it girl!" I smiled.

"Thanks." She smiled back. "Your turn."

"What did you get?" I said to Marcus.

"Straight A's." He smiled proudly. Both Elida and my mouths dropped open in shock.

Reggie went up next, but he looked at his on his way back to his seat. "Second honors," he said.

"You did not get straight A's!" said Elida, snatching Marcus' card from him. Her eyes widened as she looked at it. "You really did it!"

She handed me his card, and I looked too. "Wow, Marcus." I was so proud of him.

"You are very intelligent," said Elida.

"Thanks y'all." Marcus smiled.

"Hey, I did good too!" Reggie said, and faked a pout.

"True, good job Reggie!" I said.

"Your turn," said Elida, focusing back on me.

I had been delaying this way too long, so I handed it to Marcus. "Go head, bring me to my doom."

He unfolded the paper, looked at my grades, then looked back at me. "Hmmm." His tone and expression were unreadable.

Reggie peered over his shoulder, then looked at me. His expression was blank too.

"What is it? Is it bad? Is it all F's?"

"I don't know, Shorty." Marcus shook his head, then gave it to Elida. She looked at it, then hit Marcus in the arm. He burst out in a big smile, both of his dimples showing. My heart dropped. Elida handed me the paper.

"I couldn't resist," said Marcus, and he and Elida started laughing.

I looked at the paper. English... A. Okay, that wasn't bad. Physical Education... A. I chuckled. Algebra...C. I did my best. Biology...C. I really needed to pull my grades up. Spanish...B. Okay, things were looking up! Culinary Arts... A. History... B!

"I passed!" I exclaimed. This was the first time since middle school that there was not one 'D' or 'F' on my report card. I had truly turned over a new leaf. I was so happy. I could not wait to get home to show my mom.

"Damn girl. You look like you just won a Grammy or something," said Marcus.

"Shut up," I laughed, hitting him in his arm.

"Look, I'm not about to have y'all women abusing me." He playfully rubbed his arm.

We chilled for the rest of the period, then it was time to go home.

Daddy called me on the bus ride home. "What's the verdict, Darlin'?" he asked.

I was practically bursting with excitement. "Daddy, I did it! There were no D's and no F's!"

I heard the smile in his voice. "I knew you could do it. Send me a copy when you get a chance."

"I will. I miss you."

"I miss you too. It's not too much longer that I'll be here, then we'll see each other again."

I tried not to think about how many years he had left.

We chatted for a few more minutes, then Daddy's time was up.

"I love you!" I said.

"Love you too, Darlin'."

I got off the bus and walked to the apartment with confidence. My mother was sitting in the kitchen, reading a newspaper.

"Hey Ma!" I said, a huge smile on my face.

"What are you so goofy for?" She stared at me.

"I got my report card today."

"And?"

"See for yourself." I took it out of my backpack and handed it to her. She unfolded it and looked at it for a while.

"Well?" I finally said, feeling anxious all of a sudden.

"Well what?"

"What do you think?" My pride was starting to waver.

"This ain't shit."

The little smile I had left disappeared. "What do you mean?"

She tossed the report card onto the table. "What are you trying to prove by showing this to me? This ain't shit, just like I said. You know your stupid ass can't make no grades like this. You probably got yourself a smart little friend, and copied her shit."

I stared at her, trying not to be hurt by her words. "Ma, no I didn't. I did that work myself. I worked hard and made those grades." I fought back tears.

"Who you trying to get smart with?" She snatched up my report card and ripped it to shreds. "Now what you got? Huh?"

"Ma, why you do that?" I felt so small.

"'Cause I felt like it. Don't question me. Walking around here like you better than somebody. Bitch, your shit stink too."

"I never said I was better than nobody. And I'm not stupid." I turned to go up to my room.

"WHO DO YOU THINK YOU TALKING TO?"

I jumped at my mother's voice and turned back around. She was right in front of me, in my face.

"Ma, I'm not getting smart with you—"

She smacked me. I touched my face. It was burning. A tear escaped.

"You stupid little bitch!" She pushed me against the wall.

"I'm not stupid." I spoke in a low voice.
"What did you say?"
"I'm not stupid—"
She punched me in the jaw. I was instantly filled with pain.
"Listen here, little bitch! If I tell you ya stupid, ya stupid! You hear me?"
I didn't answer. She stepped closer, threatening to hit me again.
"Yes."
"What did I say?" Her eyes were full of hatred and rage.
"I'm stupid."
"Say it again!"
"I'm stupid!" I said a little louder.
"That's right. You stupid, and you'll never be anything but that. Now get up out of my face."

Marcus

Me, Dave, and Reggie were headed to practice after school. The first game of the season was coming up. Me and Dave most likely wouldn't get to play, but Reggie would.

"Look at you, Big Time!" Dave said, nudging Reggie.

Reggie gave off a nervous smile. "I just hope I get some points on the board."

"You will, man," I encouraged him.

"You got this," Dave said, but I saw a hint of jealousy in his eyes.

"What's been up wit that nigga E though?" Reggie asked.

I shrugged, but Dave spoke on it.

"Man, that nigga E been wilding. Ever since the day he took that kids' Jordan's, he been setting niggas up and robbing them left and right. He started hanging with Nino and them."

My jaw dropped. "What the fuck is E doing hanging with Nino?" Nino was an older guy, around nineteen or twenty years old, and he was part of one of the neighborhood gangs, RECKLESS. They had graffiti all over our side of town. There was another gang a few blocks over called The North Side, and them and RECKLESS was always going at it.

I never wanted no parts of a gang. I just wanted to stick to school, go to college, and get on with my life.

Dave shrugged before he spoke again. "He been messed up in the head ever since he didn't make the team."

Reggie cut in. "Yeah, but that don't mean he gotta get involved with all that stuff. He could have tried out next year."

Dave stood up for E. "I mean, but at the same time, since we have practice almost every day, his time with us is limited. Can't be caught slipping out there without nobody to hold you down."

I took that moment to speak my mind. "Dave, that was fucked up what he did to that kid Jeffrey though." I had learned the kid's name one day while I was taking the bus and he was on it. Jeffrey was talking to some girl and she called his name out. He looked to be in good spirits and had a fresh pair of Jordan's on, which meant his parents were probably laced.

Me, Reggie, and Dave also had Jordan's. My dad was in the military and my mom was always feeling guilty after their divorce, so she made sure I had a pair. Reggie's mom always bought him the latest gear since he was an only child. Dave was being raised by his grandmother, and one of his uncles hooked him up. E's mom was on Section 8 so she couldn't afford to buy all her kids the latest gear.

Dave looked defensive. "Look, it's not our fault Jeffrey got caught slipping. You said he got a new pair right?"

"Yes, but…"

Reggie held his hands up. "Let's just squash it and get to practice before we're late. We can't change the past."

Reggie

Even though I told Marcus and Dave to chill, I believed Marcus had a point. E was going down the wrong path. I planned to try to talk to him at some point to get his head straight.

I couldn't think about that during practice, however. Coach said we needed to keep our heads in the game. I can't front; I imagined my mom sitting in the stands cheering me on as I made multiple shots.

Coach said if I did good enough during this first game, I would get more playing time.

"You only have a few minutes to prove yourself, Reggie. Just take everything you've learned out here during practice, and give it your best."

I swallowed and nodded when he told me that.

Rex approached me after practice. Dave and Marcus were already walking toward the locker room, so they didn't realize I wasn't with them at first. "Yo Reg, you wanna hit up this party with us later on?"

It was the moment of truth.

By "us", I knew Rex meant that Dave and Marcus wouldn't be invited since they were only junior varsity. Still I would feel like shit if I didn't try.

"Can my boys come too?" I tried to put some bass in my voice as I spoke, but it came out wrong. I watched as Dave noticed my absence and turned around. Marcus did too.

Rex mocked me. "*Can my boys come too?* Look, we ain't trying to babysit. You varsity. You need to get used to that idea."

"Yeah, but..."

"But nothing. You coming or not?"

Steve, one of the other seniors, joined in the conversation. He stood there with his arms crossed, trying to see what I would do. Jamal, another upperclassman, also watched our interaction.

I couldn't do it.

I didn't know if I would regret this decision later or what, but I was sticking with my boys.

"Maybe next time. I gotta study for a test anyway."

Rex waved me off. "Whatever lil nigga."

I didn't dare respond to that one.

Elida

I was lying in bed when I got a phone call. I looked at the screen and saw Shorty's name and picture flashing. I quickly answered.
"Hello?"
"Elida..." Her voice sounded way off.
"What's going on? You okay?"
"She hated it."
"Your mom?"
"Yeah, she... hold on." She sounded like she was about to cry.
"Hello?"
I heard her sniffling.
At that moment, my brother Sammy burst into my room. "Who you on the phone with?"
"Oh my gosh, Sammy, get out!" I said, feeling myself getting angry.
"Who you talking to?" he repeated.
"None of your business, now get out!"
"I'm telling Mommy you talking to a boy!"
"No, I'm not, now get out!"

"What's your friend's name then?"
"Alize. Get out!"
"She got a big booty?"
"SAMMY, GET THE HELL OUT OF MY ROOM!" I screamed. I know my mother had to have heard me swear, and I was probably about to be in trouble, but he was just so annoying.

"Fine. Freaking cock block." He left, slamming the door.

"I'm sorry, girl." I said to Shorty. "Now, what were you saying?"

"I didn't know you had a little brother."

"Yes, and a little sister. They are both annoying at times. What's going on with you?"

"My mom made me say I was stupid."

"What?"

"She said my report card wasn't shit, and that I probably copied all my work off of somebody else."

"Are you serious?"

"Yes. Then she ripped it up."

What the hell was wrong with this girl's mother? "Wow, Shorty. I am so sorry this is happening to you." I felt powerless. It was one thing to defend your friend against random girls at school. It was a whole other thing to try to defend them against their own parent. I didn't understand how Shorty's mom could be so mean, when she worked hard to earn those grades.

"She hates me."

"Look, I don't know why your mom is acting this way, but you are not stupid. You did the work for those grades. I saw you."

"I know. She hit me."

"What?" This story was becoming too much for me.

"She smacked me, then she punched me in my jaw. She threatened to hit me again if I wouldn't say I was stupid." She broke down crying.

I felt like I didn't know what to say. I didn't know what to do in a situation like this.

"I really hope you don't believe her, Shorty." I felt totally lame that that was the best I could come up with, but I had never seen anything like this before. My mom barely ever hit us, only when we really acted up, and my dad never put his hands on me. He was never around.

"Thank you," she said softly.

How did you handle a situation like this? I thought of telling my mom, but I didn't want to get Shorty into even more trouble. I was starting to feel stressed out. I began to pray. "God, if you're listening, can you please help my friend, Shorty? I don't know why her mother is acting like this. She needs help, Lord, and I don't know how to help her."

I didn't know if my prayer would work, but I sure hoped it did.

Shorty

After I got off the phone with Elida, I felt a little better. Then my mother came upstairs to my room, threw some money at me, and told me to go to the store for her. I put on my coat and walked out the door. I felt horrible again. I was crying as I walked. I just let the tears fall down my face. I didn't even bother to wipe them because they just kept coming. I wasn't even paying attention to my surroundings. Then I bumped into something hard. I looked up. It was Marcus.

"Dang, girl. Watch where you…" He saw my face. "Shorty, what's wrong?"

I told him what happened, then I broke down again. He stood there and listened, then he wrapped his arms around me and hugged me. It felt so good. I felt safe. "It's gonna be okay, Shorty." He massaged my back. "Don't cry. It's going to be okay. I'm here for you."

"I don't know what to do to make her love me."

"You just gotta be strong. I don't know what her problem is, but if you need somebody, you know you got me. I might not be the same as like, a parent, but..."

"Thanks, Marcus. I really appreciate it." I kissed his cheek and smiled.

"See, there you go with that pretty smile." He grinned at me. Marcus could be so sweet. That's one of the reasons I like him so much. He's mad real and smart and cool and... I could go on and on about this boy. He really cared about me. It touched my heart.

When I went to science class the next morning, Janie came up and sat next to me, in Elida's seat.

"What's up, Shorty?" she said.

"Nothing." I didn't really have much to say to her since she let me get jumped. I still didn't know what to think about her, because she was definitely moving like a snake with that one.

"Really? Oh."

"How's the baby?" I decided to cut to the chase, because I had too much going on in my life and was not here for her small talk.

"What baby?" Her expression was blank.

"What do you mean, 'What baby?' The one you got me jumped for! That baby!"

"Oh." She sounded like she had forgotten all about that conversation. "I miscarried."

By this time, I was through with Janie's shenanigans. "Are you fucking kidding me? I should have known you were lying."

"Why would you think I was lying?"

"How can you be so nonchalant about losing a baby? You full of shit, Janie!"

"Look, you don't fill me in on everything in your life anymore. I didn't see the need to fill you in on everything in mine."

"Did you tell Shaneeda's man?"

"Ummm, no..." She looked at me like I had just asked a stupid question.

"Why wouldn't you at least tell him?"

"Um, it was none of his business? Why would I need to tell him?"

Now I was confused. She was looking at me like I was crazy, and I was giving her the same look.

"Didn't you tell me he was the father?"

"Ohhhh, yeah."

"Janie." I was starting to get heated now.

"What?"

"Stop fucking with me."

"I'm not fucking with you."

"Why are you acting all weird then?"

She started laughing, and that's when I noticed that her eyes were red and halfway closed. I sucked my teeth. This bitch was high!

"Janie, really?" I said in disgust.

"What?" she said, still laughing.

"You been smoking weed? Since when?"

"Since like, forever! Where have you been?"

I was so disappointed. "I thought we promised each other we would never get into all that stuff."

"Oh, quit it, Shorty."

"Quit what? I'm not joking."

"Don't act like you don't get blazed every once in a while."

"I don't. Unlike you, I keep my promises."

"Whatever." She rolled her eyes. "Why are you still hanging with that girl?"

"What girl?" This conversation was giving me a headache.

"The one who sits in this seat. You never come around me anymore. You don't stop by the house. You don't even call! What's up with that?"

"Friendship is a two-way street." I said coolly. "Last I remembered, you don't call me either, and you just got me jumped!"

"I told you why I did that."

"Yeah, but that was some snake shit. The only reason I haven't beat your ass is because I'm turning over a new leaf. Besides, I did go by your house a few times, but your mother said you been running around with some dude."

"Who? Brandon?" She started laughing again.

"I don't know. She said you be with a lot of guys. Is that true?"

She giggled. "What can I say? I get around."

"That's not funny, or cute, Janie. What, are you gonna tell me you a hoe now too?"

"Well, I'm not a virgin."

"Yeah, but I didn't know you was out there like that."

"I'm not a hoe."

"How many guys are you sleeping with?"

"I don't necessarily keep count."

"Janie..."

"What, Shorty!" She sounded like she was getting irritated with me. "Don't you freaking judge me. You've done your own dirt in your life."

"We made promises to each other, Janie."

"And promises were made to be broken." She had this faraway look in her eye when she said that. I didn't know where that was coming from.

"I don't know what you're talking about."

"Nothing. Why are you hanging with her?" She was referring to Elida again.

"She's my friend. Plus, you changed, Janie. You changed a lot. You're nothing like what you used to be."

"I'm not the one who changed. You did."

"What do you mean?"

"Look at you! You're all... smart now. You hang with freaks. You haven't been suspended since basically the beginning of the school year. You've totally lost your cool."

"You're telling me I'm not cool because I don't smoke weed, get suspended, and hoe around?" I was nearing the end point of this conversation. Janie was moving real funny, and I was on the brink of ending my friendship with her altogether.

"I don't see why you're hanging with her. It's not like she's better than me or anything."

"Janie, you really need to stop smoking that weed."

"No, you need to stop dissing your real friends for freaking weirdos!"

Just then, Elida and Marcus walked in. Reggie followed shortly after. Elida stood in front of Janie, who was still sitting in her seat.

"Um, excuse me?" Elida said, trying to be polite.

"What do you want, nerd?" said Janie, clearly not getting the memo.

"You're in my seat."

"Our seats aren't assigned. It's a free country."

"Janie." I said, trying to diffuse the situation before it became anything big.

"What?" she turned to me. "So are you going to diss me right in front of her?"

"Nobody's dissing you, but you know that's her seat."

"And like I said, the seats aren't assigned, so I don't have to move."

"Get up," said Elida, looking like she was losing patience.

"No."

"Come on, Janie!" I sighed. I really did not want to have to break up a fight between two of my friends. I hated feeling like I was in the middle.

"Get up out of my seat." Elida's eyes narrowed, like she meant business.

Janie looked back at me. My eyes pleaded for her to get up. She sucked her teeth. "I see what this is." She got up with attitude and huffed over to where she usually sat. Elida sat down.

"What's going on with her? She looks high," she whispered.

"Yes, I smoke weed, bitch! Need any more information about my life?" Janie said, shooting daggers in our direction.

Elida opened her mouth to answer, but then the teacher walked in, ready to begin the lesson.

Class was really awkward for me after that.

I feel like I'm torn between two friends. I've obviously known Janie for much longer, but she's been changing for the worst, plus she lied to me and on me, and got me jumped. It seems like a no brainer. But at the same time, I feel like something is wrong with her. Why would she all of a sudden start doing all the stuff that she said she would never do? If she was really in trouble, I couldn't just leave her hanging.

At the same time, I couldn't just diss Elida for her either.

Life is just too much.

Elida

I was sitting in my Spanish class, mad as hell. I couldn't believe that Janie girl had acted like that toward me. She had given me dirty looks and stuff before, but I've never done anything to her, so she has no reason to treat me like that.

My next class was with Marcus, but not Shorty. When he saw that I was still upset, he tried to get me to talk.

"Hey," he said.

"Hey."

"What was that all about in science?"

"I don't know why that girl is acting like that. I've done nothing to her."

"I would just leave it alone."

"I tried to be nice, but I'm not going to let her bully me."

"I understand. I think you handled it well."

That caused me to pause. Marcus was so sexy, and his compliment made me feel all weird and fluttery inside.

"Thanks." I blushed.

Marcus

When I got home, I was dog tired. I didn't want to do anything but hop in the shower and go to sleep. When I got there, however, Dad was sitting at the kitchen table with a serious expression on his face. That could only mean one thing.

"Hey Dad, what's up?"

"Hey, Son. Sit down, I need to talk to you." He gestured toward the seat across from him.

I sat.

"You look tired. How was practice?"

"It was good. We got a game coming up soon."

Dad gave me a half-smile, then it erased. "Unfortunately I won't be able to make your game."

My heart dropped. "What you mean?"

He sighed. "I'm getting deployed."

"Again?" Dad had just gotten deployed last year too.

"It's not as long this time."

"How long, Dad?"

He looked at me like he felt guilty. "Six months."

I blew out a breath and sat back. "Why do they keep doing this?"

I felt the tension rising within me. I already had a feeling what he was going to say next.

"I'm leaving this weekend, so you will have to stay with your mother again."

"Dad, please. Just let me stay here."

He blinked. "Alone?"

"Yes! I'll be fine. I know how to lock the door, I'll stay on top of my grades, and I travel with my boys to and from school. I don't need Mom."

I hadn't meant my words to come out like that, but they did.

"Marcus..." he began.

"Not like that," I said, though we both knew exactly what I meant.

"Your mother's sorry, Marcus."

"I know, but I can handle myself."

"You're only fourteen."

"Yes, but I promise you I'll be good. If I run into any issues, I'll call Mom."

He was contemplating it, I could tell.

Finally, he spoke again.

"I'll talk it over with her and see what she says. If she agrees, fine. But Marcus, I'm going to make myself crystal clear: if I come back to this house and everything is not exactly how I left it, I'm gonna beat your motherfucking ass."

He stared at me for a second, then we both burst into laughter.

"Yes Sir," I said, giving him a salute.

That last part of his sentence was a running joke between us. I was a good kid, so Dad never really had to whoop me like that. But he always joked that he would when he meant business.

"I'm gonna miss you, Son." His expression grew wistful and a tear came to his eyes.

I swallowed my emotions back too.

"I'll miss you too, Dad."

Reggie

Tonight was the night.
 Pure adrenaline was coursing through everybody's veins; I could feel it. We were going against one of our biggest rivals, and Coach said that since I did good in practice, he was definitely giving me some playing time.

I was shitting bricks, but at the same time, ready for the challenge.

Marcus and Dave cheered me on. I wish they could play too, but junior varsity players only got time on the court if something major happened like an injury.

I felt like a celebrity when they called our team out and everybody in the stands was clapping and shouting our names. Shorty and Elida came through. I was thinking of seeing if Marcus and Dave wanted to take them out to eat after.

E was supposed to be coming too, but he been mad wishy-washy lately.

Just as I had the thought, I spotted E in the crowd with Nino and his crew.

Our eyes met and he nodded. I nodded as well.

Nino yelled something and clapped roughly, but I couldn't make out his words.

I gave him a nod and wave too so he wouldn't misinterpret me. The last thing I needed was Nino and his crew feeling any type of way about me. I wasn't in the gang, which basically meant I should be fair game to the streets, but since E was down, I was down by extension as long as no bullshit happened.

It seemed like I blinked and the game was already underway.

I spent the whole first quarter with my eyes running back and forth between the clock, the teams, and the stands.

My mom was standing in the crowd with our school colors, black and silver on. Her face was all made up and she had on a silver wig.

She looked ridiculous, but I know she did it for me.

I had to make her proud tonight.

Finally, my time came to shine.

When Coach called my name and told me to go in to replace this kid named Rell, I almost threw up. I scanned the crowd for my mom again, and when she saw me walking onto the court, she screamed and jumped up and down.

I heard her loud ass from where I was on the court.

I couldn't front. It made me smile.

I wished my dad was there, but before he passed away a few years ago, he told me to be a man and make my mother proud.

"Stay out of trouble, go to college or learn a trade, and raise up as the man I know you can be. Always look out for your mother. Treat the ladies right. I'll be looking down, making sure you stay out of trouble."

I blinked back a tear to focus back on the game.

Cancer was a motherfucker.

My five minutes on the court went by like a whirlwind.

At first, it was mainly just running back and forth, guarding my guy while Rex had the ball. Then out of nowhere, he passed it to me.

I caught it and took the open shot without even thinking.

My eyes widened with surprise as it sailed clean through the hoop. It felt surreal, but the thunderous applause from the crowd let me know that that really just happened.

A couple minutes later, I got the ball again and crossed this dude up to make another shot. The crowd went crazy. I was on fire after that, and I was able to make a three-pointer right before Coach took me out the game.

"Enjoy the rush!" he yelled at me over the crowd. "You'll get used to it soon enough."

He winked, and my heart warmed.

He was going to let me get more playing time! I couldn't believe it. My very first game as a varsity player, and I had seven points on the board.

During the final quarter, Jamal went down.

His knee got injured so they had him sit out. He looked pissed. I would have been pissed too. I thought Coach was going to put me back in, but he called Marcus instead.

Part of me felt a little jealous, but another part was happy to see my boy get some shine too. Like I said before, junior varsity only got playing time under special circumstances.

Marcus ended up scoring two points. I knew he was happy about that.

After Coach took Marcus out, he let Dave jump in. Dave didn't score any points, but I could tell he was riding the wave of just being on the court while the crowd was cheering him on. He blocked one of the other team's shots, so he got some clout for that too.

Almost immediately after the game, Rex approached me.

"Guess you and your boys earned some stripes tonight."

I couldn't help but grin.

"Y'all want to hit up a party with us?"

I couldn't believe my ears. I looked at Dave and Marcus. "Y'all down?"

"Hell yeah!" Dave said.

We all got excited and my mom brought us back to the neighborhood to get ready to celebrate our big win. Rex was picking us up later.

Shorty

I got home from the game to see my mom's ex boyfriend, Ronald sitting on the couch.
"What are you doing here?" I asked, before I could stop myself.
"Ain't your Momma teach you manners?" he joked.
"You guys are back together?"
He smirked. "We're working on it. Why? You tryina see something?"
That wasn't a joke.
And it was exactly why I wished my mom left Ronald's nasty ass in the dust.
"Is she coming back soon?" I thought about going to my aunt's house until she returned.
Ronald didn't have to answer.
The key turned in the lock and my mom entered the apartment.
"I see you know how to follow directions," she said to me.

She had told me to be home by 10:00pm. I made sure I did, because there was no telling what would happen if I didn't.

"How was your day?" I asked.

"Good. Go to your room so me and Ronald can have some privacy."

I was about to say something but I didn't. I just went up to my room and closed the door, hoping Ronald wasn't staying the night.

When I got in my room, my phone buzzed with a text from Janie. *That game was dope right?*

My jaw dropped. *You were there? I didn't see you.*

Of course I was there. I'm a student too, you know.

Right. Anyway, WYD.

Nothing. Want to hang this weekend?

I paused before I answered. I still wasn't over what Janie did to me, but at the same time, I felt bad about her argument with Elida, and it being seen as me taking Elida's side.

I decided to give in.

Sure. Just let me know when.

Elida

I was walking down the street toward our house from the bus stop when a car pulled up beside me. At first I got scared, but my heart leapt with excitement when the window rolled down and I saw that it was Daddy.

"Hey, Baby Girl," he said.

"Daddy, what are you doing here? We miss you!"

He gave me a pained smile. "I miss you and your brother and sister too, Elida."

"Are you coming in? Mommy's probably not home yet, but..."

My smile faltered as Daddy shook his head.

"Not today, Honey, but check me out: I plan to see you guys this weekend."

"Yeah?" All my excitement had gone out the window by now, because at this point it was clear that Daddy wasn't really coming. I could tell by his body language.

"Absolutely." He smiled again. "I just had a question though. My tank is a little low, and I've got to get to work. Do you have a few dollars I could hold until I get paid?"

I thought about it. Mommy had just given us allowance yesterday. I had $20, while Sammy and Gabriella got $10 each.

I usually used my allowance to get nachos at lunch time, but if Daddy needed to get to work, that was more important.

"Sure!" I said, and pulled out my wallet. I handed Daddy the bill with pride.

"Thank you, Baby Girl," he said. "I'm going to head to work now, but you be good okay?"

I nodded. "Yes, Daddy."

I waved as he drove off, then let myself into our house. Sammy and Gabriella wouldn't be getting off their bus for another hour. I usually met them at the corner and walked them down.

I made myself a snack and watched some TV in the meantime.

A few hours later, Mommy came home while we were all watching a movie.

"Did you kids do your homework?" she asked.

"Yes," I answered for my siblings. "I made sure they did. I did mine too. Oh, Mommy guess what? Daddy stopped by today."

Mommy froze. "Stopped by? When?"

I told her what happened, and as soon as I finished, I could tell something was wrong.

"He said what?" Her eyes narrowed. "And he actually took your allowance?"

I was confused. "He needed it to get to work."

"That motherf..." Mommy caught herself before she swore. She huffed upstairs to her bedroom and slammed the door.

A few moments later, we heard her yelling on the phone at Daddy.

I tried to focus on the movie, but it was hard to. My heart was filled with guilt.

Finally the yelling stopped, and Mommy called me to her room.

"Yes?" I said, standing at her door.

"Here," she said, and handed me another $20 bill. "You take this, and don't you ever give your father any money again. Understand?"

"Why?"

"Don't worry about why, Elida. Just don't do it, okay?"

"Are you mad at me?"

"No, I'm not mad at you. It's your father who should be... Never mind. Just go finish your movie."

I went back to the living room, and Sammy had the remote in his hand. Apparently, he had paused the movie to see what Mommy was going to say to me.

He gave me a look of disgust when I sat back next to him.

"You should have never said anything! Now Daddy will never come back." He tossed the remote to the other couch and went upstairs to his room. Gabriella was just silent.

I noticed that she had been silent a lot lately.

I felt horrible.

Marcus

Jamal is going to have to sit out for the next few weeks, so Coach said there's a chance me and Dave may get even more playing time. It was lit to even be considered since we were only JV. Of course, he would probably play some other junior varsity members too, but me and Dave were considered to be some trendsetters since we paved the way.

Me, Reggie, and Dave met up at E's apartment.

We decided to play some video games at his crib since we hadn't got up with him in a while.

Reggie knocked, and E opened the door to let us in. Immediately, the smell of weed almost overtook me. I started coughing.

"Damn, E! It's like that?" I said.

We made our way to his living room, where I froze up immediately. Nino and two of his boys, Larry and Dawan were sitting on the couch.

I could tell from Reggie's expression he wasn't expecting to see them either.

Dave looked nonchalant.

Nino laughed at my response to the weed. "E, nigga. Why your boy so uptight?"

E chuckled. "I told you my boys is kind of square."

That pissed me off, but I wasn't about to say anything.

Larry started rolling up more weed, while Nino extended his blunt to Reggie. "Here you go, Mr. Star Player. We seen you out there on the court."

Reggie looked nervous. "Oh, I don't smoke, man."

Nino wasn't hearing him.

"Matter of fact, how about all y'all hit it?"

I shot a glance at Reggie, then Dave.

Dave moved first to take the blunt from Nino's hand.

He started coughing almost immediately.

Nino and Larry burst out laughing. "You right E; these young niggas square as fuck!"

Dave handed it to me.

I didn't want anything to do with marijuana, since I did a report on its effects on the adolescent brain for my science class, but I had no idea what Nino would do if I didn't, especially with the way his eyes were daring me to say no.

I took the blunt, but I tried to indulge as minimally as possible so I wouldn't get high. My dad was already gone on his deployment, and my mom agreed to let me stay at the house as long as she could pop in whenever she wanted, so I was good. Hopefully she didn't choose tonight as one of her nights to check in.

Once Nino looked satisfied with me, I handed it to Reggie.

He handed it back to Nino, and I immediately felt like a little bitch.

"Nah, I'm good," Reggie said.

Nino eyed Reggie, then stood.

I could tell Reggie was nervous, but he was trying to stand his ground at the same time.

I moved closer to Reggie in case anything popped off.

It was crazy to me that E invited Nino and them in the first place, much less let him basically force drugs on us. His loyalty was shifting, I could tell.

"One hit won't hurt you," Nino said, staring Reggie in his eyes.

We all could tell that he meant a whole lot more with his words than he said.

Reggie swallowed.

I knew he didn't want to do it, but when Nino held the blunt out again, he took it.

He stared Nino in the eyes as he puffed it twice, then handed it back.

Nino stared at him for a few more seconds, then chuckled.

"I like this one."

We thought it was over after that, but as the video game continued, Nino and his boys kept passing us the blunt. I was starting to feel extremely nauseous, but I didn't want to show it. Dave just kept laughing uncontrollably, and Reggie looked more and more uncomfortable.

About an hour into the game, one of E's sisters, Shalaysia came bursting out of her room. "Ew, that smell is nasty!"

"Go back to your room!" E barked at her.

"I'm telling Mommy!"

"And I'll beat your ass."

Shalaysia's eyes welled up. "We're hungry." E had three younger sisters, all of them likely in that same room. E went to the kitchen, grabbed some cookies from the top of the refrigerator, juice containers from inside it, and handed them to her. "Eat this. Mommy will be home soon."

Shalaysia took the food and closed the door.

Reggie looked more and more pissed through their whole interaction. "Yo, I gotta go," he said abruptly. He handed E his controller.

"Why you leaving so early?" E asked.

Reggie didn't answer. He just headed for the door. I hopped up and followed him, then turned back. "Dave, you coming?"

Dave looked between Nino and his crew, E, and us.

"Nah man, y'all go ahead."

Me and Reggie left.

Reggie

I couldn't believe I bitched out like that. Part of me wasn't scared of Nino, but another part was. I had to get the hell out of E's house.

"Yo man, wait up!" Marcus said as he jogged to catch up with me. I guess I was walking kind of fast.

"You alright man?" I asked him.

He shook his head. "Not really." He dropped his head as we walked at a slower pace. "If my dad was home, he would have killed me."

"I can only imagine what my mom is gonna do."

As soon as I finished my sentence, Marcus suddenly jerked forward, then covered his mouth with his hand.

"You good?" I asked, my mind swimming from the high.

Vomit poured through his fingers as my response. I thought quick.

"Come on man, let's go to the corner store."

We went to the store, and Marcus headed to the bathroom to wash his face and hands while I went to grab us some spray, eye drops, snacks, and drinks.

When he came out of the bathroom, I was ready to go.

"Can we chill at your house for a few? I don't want my mom seeing me like this."

Marcus nodded, and we headed to his crib.

When we got inside, he flipped on the light and plopped onto the couch. "You didn't feel like throwing up?" he asked me.

I shook my head. "I was more pissed off than anything. I feel like a fucking bitch."

"Nigga, at least you stood up for yourself. I caved immediately."

We sat in silence for a second while I downed two bottles of Gatorade back to back, then ate some brownies.

Marcus ate and drank too, then he spoke up. "I'm not fucking with that nigga E no more. I feel like he crossed the line tonight."

I nodded. "I agree. I mean, I still see him as a friend, but I'm not going to his house no more."

Marcus sat there for another second. "Right."

We chilled for another hour, then I used the eye drops and sprayed myself down to try to eliminate the smell. I also took the longer route home. It was kind of tough to do since me and Marcus' apartments was only a few buildings from each other in the complex, but I tried my best to make the wind eliminate the rest of the smell.

It didn't work.

As soon as I got in the house, my mother stopped me.

"Unh uh, Reggie. What is that smell?"

She hopped up from her position on the couch.

"Answer me!"

I tried to think of a reply. "It's nothing, Ma."

I felt the slap before I saw her hand.

"Reggie, you know way better than that! You will not be smoking weed while living under my roof. We talked about this. You know I…"

I zoned out while my mother was talking.

There was no need for her speech. I already made my decision to steer clear of E.

Shorty

I've been trying my best to keep my head down and stay out of trouble at school and at home. I hung out with Janie once or twice, but I feel like our relationship just isn't the same.

I don't know if it's because of the whole jumping incident or there really is a distance between us now. I decided to just put that relationship on the backburner for now.

Ronald basically moved back in.

After that first night, he started coming over every other day, then he finally moved a couple of suitcases in and stopped leaving, except to go to work.

I can't stand his ass, but my mom doesn't seem to have any inkling about what he's doing behind her back.

Tonight is the last game of the season. Me and Elida are going. I thought about texting Janie even though I wasn't really fucking with her, but I decided against it.

I wasn't about to have her saying something crazy, then having to break up a fight between her and Elida. Janie made it clear she really doesn't like her for some reason.

Be home by 11:00pm, my mother texted.

Okay, I texted back, then slipped my phone in my back pocket. I was excited to see the boys play. Reggie done turned himself into a superstar with all the points he has racked up over the season, and the coach also let Marcus play a few more times too, until Jamal got better.

The rumor around school is that Jamal was healed enough to play tonight.

I guess we would see.

"Hey!" Elida said, looking excited to see me.

We hugged.

"Black and silver, girl!" I said to her.

She was wearing a black and silver hoodie with our school's team name on it.

I had on a regular black hoodie with silver earrings.

We got some good seats and settled in for the game.

Pretty soon, it was time for the boys to run out.

"Marcus! Reggie! Whoo!" I shouted.

Elida shouted too.

Marcus saw us and waved.

Reggie did too.

We could feel the anticipation throughout the room because if we won this game, we won the championship. Our team had been mostly undefeated the whole season.

"Girl, I hope we get it!" Elida said, grinning from ear to ear.

"Me too!"

And we did. Reggie scored 18 points. Jamal did get to play, so Marcus had to sit out the most of the game, but the coach let him jump in during the last quarter when it was clear we were winning and he scored a shot.

The crowd went wild.

"LET'S GO FRESHMEN, LET'S GO!" The cheerleaders started, then the crowd picked up the chant. During the last few seconds of the game, the team captain, Rex, scored the final points, bringing his total points during the game to 22.

It was then that I realized just how good Reggie was.

"Girl, Reggie almost beat Rex!" I said to Elida.

Her eyes widened too. "Right!"

After the game, we hung with Marcus, Reggie, and their boy Dave for a few moments before they were whisked away by Coach Rivers to celebrate.

"Oh shoot, we gotta catch the bus!" I said, and me and Elida started running for the stop.

Unfortunately, we just missed it.

I looked at my phone and became frantic. It was after 10:30, and my mom said to be home by 11:00pm.

"OMG..." I said to Elida.

"Here comes another one!" she said.

We got on and chatted until Elida's stop came. She lived in a different part of the city from me, but both of our houses were right near the stops, so we were good.

I watched her race to her front door as the bus pulled off, then I sat back in my seat, checking my phone again.

It was 10:51pm, and my stop was ten minutes away.

Almost home, I texted my mom, but she didn't respond.

The bus dropped me off at 11:00pm on the dot.

I rushed toward my apartment and unlocked the door, ready to apologize for being a couple minutes late. I unlocked the door, but was blocked by the chain.

"Ma!" I called out. "Ma!"

She approached the door a few moments later. "Yes?"

"I missed the first bus, but one came right after. Sorry for being late."

"Well now you have to face the consequences."

My heart dropped. "What do you mean?"

"You're not coming in."

I protested. "Ma, it's only 11:07. I got here as fast as I could."

"Should have made the first bus." She moved to close the door.

"Ma, it's cold!"

She closed it and re-locked it.

My mind began swimming. What was I going to do? I shivered due to a cold gust of wind. Then I remembered my Auntie Gina lived a couple of doors down. I prayed that she was home. My eyes scanned the parking lot for her car, and it was there.

I went to her door and knocked.

"Auntie!"

She opened it.

"Girl, what are you doing at my house this late?"

"My mom won't let me in."

She looked surprised. "Won't let you in? Why not?"

I shrugged. "I got home late."

She stared at me for a few moments.

"Come on in, Alize."

Elida

Sammy came to my room door while I was doing my best rendition of the latest Jhene Aiko song. "You know you can't sing," he said.

"Shut up," I said back.

"Mommy wants us."

"For what?"

He shrugged. "I don't know. Just come on."

I decided not to put up a fight since Sammy only recently started talking to me again. He was super mad that day Mommy called Daddy and yelled at him.

We hadn't seen Daddy since then, but Sammy got over his anger when I kept letting him choose the show or movie we watched until Mommy got home from work.

We got to Mommy's room, and Gabriella was already in there.

"What's this about?" Sammy asked, plopping on her bed.

"Elida, you sit too," Mommy instructed.

I sat between my siblings. Mommy's bed was a posture-pedic.

"I want to share something with you guys."

"What is it?" Gabriella's eyes lit up.

Mommy looked kind of nervous. "Well as you all know, I met a new friend."

I already didn't like where this conversation was going. By friend, I knew she was referring to Mr. Loser, her boyfriend.

"What about him?" Sammy asked, getting defensive.

"I want you three to meet him."

"No!" Gabriella said, taking the words out of me and Sammy's mouths.

Mommy shot her a stern look. "Watch your mouth, little girl."

Gabriella calmed down slightly in response.

"Why do we have to meet him?" Sammy asked.

"Because he might be a part of the family soon."

"Part of the family?!" I said before I could help myself. "How so?"

"We're thinking of getting married."

"Mommy, you can't!" Gabriella said. "What about Daddy?"

Mommy's expression softened. "Gabby, honey, me and your daddy both love you, but sometimes relationships between parents don't work out."

"Whatever," Sammy said, and hopped off the bed to leave.

"Hey!" Mommy said.

He stopped. "What?"

"You better fix your face and that attitude before you get yourself in trouble."

Sammy calmed down, but still went to his room.

Mommy looked at me, while Gabriella sniffled, then burst into tears.

I opened my mouth to say congratulations to Mommy, but decided against it because I knew it wouldn't be genuine.

Marcus

Time has been flying by. Summer is almost here. Dad should be back by July, and I've been missing him like crazy. My mom keeps popping up a couple times a week, and it's more annoying than anything.

Seems like she can't take a hint.

"Hi, Marcus!" she said, opening my blinds one Saturday morning.

I groaned and looked at my alarm clock.

"Mom, it's only seven o'clock!" I wished Dad didn't give her a key to the apartment. She saw no problem with invading my privacy by busting up in my room whenever she felt the need.

She chuckled. "Well it's time for you to wake up. We're hanging out today."

"Hanging out? I had plans with some friends."

Me, Reggie, Elida, and Shorty were supposed to get up.

"Well you're going to have to cancel."

"Mom, you can't just do things like this."

"Things like what? Be your mother?"

I paused. I was not trying to go down this road today.

"Marcus, I have apologized a million times to you. We need to get past this." Her arms were crossed.

"I don't want to talk about it."

"Well, we're going to. Today. We've been avoiding this conversation for too long. I am your mother."

I felt myself growing uneasy. "I forgive you, but I really did have plans today."

"No, you don't forgive me, Marcus. I see it all over your face every time I come here. You think I was shocked you didn't want to come stay with me during your father's deployment? What I did was wrong, but everybody makes mistakes. Even parents."

She was really trying to do this.

"If it was such a mistake, why did you marry him after?"

My mom had cheated on my dad during one of his deployments. He found out when he came home early and caught them in bed together. I was at school, but I put two and two together when I heard them arguing about it later that day.

She swore up and down that she was sorry, but a few months later, she was asking for a divorce and marrying the other dude. I don't speak his name. Fuck him.

"Marcus, Felix is a good man. Things didn't work out with your father, and once again I'm sorry, but we gotta get over this hump."

"The way I see it, you chose him when you left us."

My mother looked like I just slapped her in the face.

She stayed silent for a few moments, then slowly turned to leave.

I didn't follow.

Reggie

This year was crazy. I had no idea coming in that during my freshman year, I would gain so many friends and even get some clout due to my spot on the varsity team.

I couldn't wait to see what next year would bring.

My mom said she was proud of me when she saw my final report card. I knew Dad would have been proud too. Mom was worried about me for a minute after the whole weed situation, but I kept my promise to myself to never go to E's house again.

We still hung out from time to time, with me, him, Dave, and Marcus, but I don't like the effect E is having on Dave. Granted, Dave and E were always tighter than me and Marcus, but still, Dave does better when E's not around.

I know that sounds fucked up, but I gotta call it how I see it.

Shorty

This year was pretty rough. I'm trying to keep focus, but sometimes it's really hard with everything that's been going on. We made it to the end, and I passed all my classes, thank God. But of course, the fact that I actually passed everything had absolutely no effect on my mother. She's still with Ronald's stankin ass, and of course, he makes his slick comments to me whenever she's not around.

I think I'm going to try to get a summer job to stay the hell away from him. He's always going to be around the house now, and I don't want to deal with it.

There are very limited options for jobs for people who are only fifteen (my birthday recently passed), but I am determined to get something, because I can't be in that house. They have a hiring event at Unique Amusements, and they are taking on a very small number of 14 and 15 year olds. I applied the other day, and I really, really hope I get it. My only other option that I know of is the library.

I'm still worried about Janie.

Ever since the incident at the mall, our friendship has become more and more distant.

Elida

Well, this year was definitely a change for me. I made some friends and I turned over a new leaf as far as not letting people bully me anymore.

Shorty is still friends with that Janie girl. I can't stand her, honestly. Every time I see her, she gives me a dirty look. She doesn't say much, but I can tell she can't stand me, and I can't stand her either.

Marcus is as fine as can be.

I think I'm kind of developing a crush on him, but I have a feeling that Shorty low-key likes him too. I hope not, because that would just make life even more complicated.

I guess we will see.

Shorty

Elida and I were sitting in Organic Chemistry when Marcus walked in looking heated. He sat and put his head down on his desk. Elida and I looked at each other, then back at him. We had never seen Marcus this upset before.

"What's wrong?" Elida asked.

"Nothing." He kept his head down.

"Then why are you acting like you are depressed or something?" I asked. "Come on, Marcus. You've been there for us – let us be here for you."

He put his head up and looked at Elida for a few seconds, then at me. "It's just that... niggas be hating."

"About...?" I said.

"Yesterday, I was chilling with Reggie, Dave, and E. Dave and E were all smoking weed and shit. E asked me if I wanted some. I said no. Then they started laughing at me. I said, 'The fuck is so funny?' Then Dave started getting on me, saying that I was a goody two shoes, like I'm some kind of punk. He said I don't belong in the hood because I don't act like I'm from here. E said I act like I'm some burbs type nigga."

"Wow, that's messed up, Marcus!" I said. I looked at Elida. "All of us live in the same hood. We grew up together. For Dave and them to be saying something like this is crazy. Marcus don't belong? They bugging!"

I low-key felt some type of way, not only for Marcus, but also for myself. Janie had been pretty much saying the same thing to me last year, and we barely saw each other over the summer, especially with my summer job and stuff. I hated that people we grew up with were starting to see us like we are totally different now.

"I told them that I grew up the same way they did. I lived in the same hood since birth. Just 'cause I don't wanna smoke weed don't make me a sellout."

"You're absolutely right," said Elida.

"I just feel messed up because Dave and E been my boys for as long as I can remember. We literally grew up together, played together, fought together, everything. And now this is how they treat me?"

"Wow, Marcus," I repeated. "I'm sorry to hear this is happening to you."

Elida

I feel really sorry for Marcus. I don't really know Dave and E – I mean, I only see them here and there in school since we didn't have any classes together last year, but from what I'm hearing, they sound like terrible friends.

I think they may just be jealous of him or something, because he really doesn't deserve to be treated like he doesn't belong, just because he is different. That is totally not fair. After reflecting on Marcus' situation, a new poem came to me.

I know you probably figured I was finished writing since I finally have friends now, but it's still a passion of mine, and a way to release. Here it is:

What I Do

I gave up too many, plenty of times
But then I keep goin', writing plenty of rhymes
I want to make it someday; they say, how silly am I?
But once I heard that if I keep looking, I'll find

What do I wanna be? What's my place in this world?

Am I gonna be the one who says 'dumb' or 'absurd'?

Locked up in a cage, or flying free like a bird?

Take it one step at a time, or all you see is a blur?

I'm just doing my thing, creating my path

I ain't no different than you just 'cause I'm passing this class

Don't get mad at me 'cause mine ain't the life you would choose

And when I succeed, don't hate on me 'cause you chose to LOSE.

Does that sound messed up? I mean, I'm not trying to put anyone down, but I do believe sometimes that we have a choice as to how our lives turn out. I keep thinking back to how those girls used to bully me, and I would just take it, but then last year, when Janie tried to do the same, I blanked out on her, and she hasn't tried me since.

It's kind of empowering, but also kind of depressing that you really have to go through all that just to get people to not feel like they can walk all over you.

Oh well; I guess it's just a part of life.

Marcus

Me, Reggie, Elida, and Shorty were hanging over Reggie's house. His mom let us chill in the basement and made us some snacks, while she was upstairs in the living room.

We were currently involved in a fierce game of UNO.

I glanced around the card table. Elida had three cards left, Shorty had five, and Reggie had two. I still had three. It was Elida's turn, and I had a hunch what she was gonna do, but if she did, I had something for her ass.

Just as I thought, she threw down a Draw Four.

"Sorry," she said, not looking sorry at all. She stuck out her tongue for emphasis.

"What color?" I demanded.

"Blue."

"BAM!" I threw down a blue Draw Two.

Reggie looked pissed. "Bullshit! You can't throw a Draw Two on top of a Draw Four."

"Yes you can," me and Shorty said in unison.

I nodded at her. My girl always had my back.

"I don't think that's in the rules, Marcus," said Elida.

I faked a jaw drop. "What? Elida, he's about to win!"

"I know, but if it's fair and square..."

"You heard the lady," Reggie said. "Retract that card, Peasant."

"Forget that. Let's Google it."

I whipped out my phone. Reggie did the same.

"Ha!" he said, finding the result first. He held out his phone.

"Whatever," I said. I held out my phone as well.

Both of our sites said the opposite.

Elida jumped in. "Well on the official UNO site, it says..."

I held my hand up. "Excuse me woman, men are talking."

She cocked her head at me. "I'm sorry?"

I licked my lips.

Reggie wasn't backing down.

"Look bruh. Don't be a sore loser. Pick the card back up."

I was pissed, but I did what he said, then I drew my four cards in misery.

Reggie slapped down a blue card.

"UNO!" He and Elida shouted at the top of their lungs.

"No, I said it first!" Elida said.

Reggie chuckled. "How quickly you shifted loyalties."

"Hey, I'm trying to win too," she said.

Reggie and Elida looked at Shorty.

"You call it," Reggie said to her.

"Why can't I call it?" I asked, but Reggie ignored me.

Shorty paused. "As much as it pains me to say it, Reggie said his like a millisecond faster."

"Ugh!" Elida said, then pouted in her seat.

Shorty

I was walking through the park on the way to the store the following Saturday when I heard Reggie calling my name. "SHORTY!" he shouted. I turned and saw him running toward me. "Wait up, Ma," he said, catching up to where I was. "What's up?" He tried to hug me, but I pushed him away.

"Unh uh," I said.

"What you mean, girl?" He looked confused.

"Not smelling like that."

"Whatever. I smell like Versace."

I rolled my eyes. "Anyway, where you coming from?"

"I was just chilling with Marcus at his house."

"Oh, what were y'all doing?"

"Minding our business." He raised his eyebrows.

"Don't get smart. Why did you rush over to me?"

"Damn, I can't say hi?"

"Hi." I continued walking.

"Wait!" he blurted out.

I turned. "What?"

"I need to ask you something."

"Ask me what?"

He looked nervous all of a sudden. "Ask you if you want to talk to me." When he spoke, all of his words tumbled out all at once, like it was one long word.

I toyed with him. "Talk to you? We're talking right now."

"I mean as more than friends."

I could tell he was nervous, but I was taken aback. "Are you serious?"

"Yeah, I been feeling you for a while, girl." He put his arm around me, but I snorted and pushed him away.

"Boy, I know you ain't coming at me with that weak ass game."

"Come on, Ma. I'm trying here." He smiled.

I could tell by the look in his eyes that he really did have a crush on me. I was kind of shocked, because I never thought of Reggie that way, but now that I took a second look at him, he was hella fine! How come I never saw this before? Reggie had dimples that were even sexier than Marcus's, and he had these hazel eyes that made you just want to stare at him for days. His lips also looked smooth like butter.

All of a sudden, I was definitely feeling Reggie.

"So, what's poppin'?" he asked, still looking nervous.

"Hmm…" I still felt like messing with him.

"Girl, stop playing. You want some of this Sexy Chocolate, or nah?"

I rolled my eyes. "Shut up. I guess so."

Reggie faked like he was pissed. "You guess so? Girl don't act like you don't feel blessed by my mere presence."

"Your mere presence? You definitely tried it."

"Gimme your phone."

I cut my eyes at him. "Why?"

"Just let me see."

I handed it to him, and he typed something in, then handed it back to me with a smirk.

I looked at what he wrote and rolled my eyes at him once again. "Really, Reggie?" He had changed his name in my contacts to "Sexy Chocolate, AKA Bae."

"What? That's my name."

"I'm done with you. Give me your phone now."

He did, and I revised my own contact info.

He wrinkled his nose when he read it. "Alize Henderson? Damn, I can't even call you Shorty?"

I laughed. "You're on a trial period."

"Anyway, where were you on your way to?"

"I was gonna get some snacks from the corner store." I pointed in the direction to where I was originally headed.

"Oh cool. I'll walk you."

We laughed and joked on the way to the store, then we went in to get some snacks. To my surprise, Reggie actually paid for mine! It was only $10, but I was still cheesing because I thought that was so sweet. I would have to do something nice for him now. After we left the store, he walked me home.

Later on that night, we texted back and forth, flirting the whole time. After we had said our 'good nights', it finally hit me that I wasn't supposed to be with Reggie – I still had a crush on Marcus!

I didn't know how it had slipped my mind so easily. Reggie just came in and swept me up off my feet. I felt so disloyal, but at the same time, I kind of did like Reggie now. I wasn't sure who I actually wanted to be with more – Marcus, or Reggie?

How did life get complicated so quick?

Reggie

I was surprised Shorty never saw none of my hints after all this time. I been feeling her like crazy ever since freshman year and trying to show my interest, but she never said anything.

When I was over Marcus' house, I confessed my feelings for her, and he dared me to ask her out.

So I did, and it went even better than I hoped.

I feel like my life is complete at fifteen years old. I got my varsity spot solidified as a sophomore, got my first real girlfriend as Shorty, and me and Marcus are tighter than ever.

Life is good.

Elida

My doorbell rang. I went to answer it, and to my surprise, it was Shorty!
"Girl, what you doing here?"
"I gotta tell you something!" She was grinning from ear to ear.
I let her in. "How did you get here?" I said as we made our way to my room.
"I took an Uber." She sat on my bed.
"So what happened?" I asked, wondering what she could possibly have to tell me that had her coming all the way over to my house.
"Reggie asked me out. We're talking now."
"Reggie?" I was shocked. "How did that happen?" I struggled to process this situation. How did she end up with Reggie? It felt weird.
"Girl, I was on my way to the store, and he yelled out my name. I waited for him to catch up with me, then he was trying to hug me. I pushed him away to be a jerk. He got all nervous, then asked if we could talk. I was caught off guard, because I never saw him that way, but then I

thought about it, and Reggie is mad fine! So I said yes."

"Wow!" I wasn't sure how to take this. I mean, I was happy for my friend, definitely, but a part of me felt kind of jealous. Shorty always had guys looking at her and trying to talk to her. But no one looked at me, and no one tried to talk to me. "Congratulations!" I managed, trying not to sound salty.

"Girl, now we got to get you a man, so we can double date! Reggie and I are supposed to go to the movies this weekend."

I swallowed. "I hope you guys have fun."

"We will. Maybe we can see if Dave wants to come! I would say E, but he has a nasty attitude. Dave is much cooler, though he also has his ways."

"Um, no thanks."

"Why not? You don't want to go?"

"Shorty..." I tried to find a way to tell her this. "Guys just don't like me like that."

She looked confused. "What do you mean?"

"They don't approach me like they do for you. I have never had a guy even ask for my number."

"Well, girl, we got to get you out there! You are so beautiful – we will find you someone in no time!"

A thought of Marcus flashed through my mind, but I ignored it. "We'll see." I really had no faith whatsoever that Shorty could find me a man, but I wasn't trying to kill her vibe.

"Are you a virgin?" she blurted out.

"Yeah. Are you?"

She nodded. "You ever kissed a boy?"

I shook my head. "Nope."

"I have." She chuckled. "What's weird is, Marcus was actually my first kiss."

When she said those words, I suddenly felt hot all over. The walls felt like they were closing in on me. So not only did Reggie like Shorty, but Marcus too? This was starting to be too much for me.

"Marcus was your first kiss?" was all I could get out without letting her see my feelings.

"Yeah, it was during a game of 'Truth or Dare' when we were like thirteen."

"Oh, wow." I tried to play it off. Age thirteen was only two years ago, since we were fifteen now.

"Girl, who do you like? We got to get you kissed!"

I blushed nervously. I wanted to say Marcus, but Shorty had just shared that he was her first kiss, so I didn't have anyone else to name. "I don't know."

"Girl, I know you like somebody."

"Well... I do, but..."

"Okay." She looked at me expectantly. "Then who?"

"Marcus." I looked away. When I looked back, I could see that her expression had changed slightly, like she was kind of surprised, and also kind of upset.

"Oh, really?"

"Yeah. But I didn't mention it before because I didn't know if you also liked him."

"Well I ain't gonna lie. I do like Marcus, a lot. But..."

"Then I'm not even gonna try him."

"Why not? I mean, if he likes you, then why not? It's not like there's anything I could do about it. Plus I'm with Reggie."

I agreed with her, but I also didn't want to cause drama in our friendship. "No, I wouldn't do that to you. If you like him, I wouldn't try to be with him."

"Are you sure? Because I could just get over it."

"No, I don't want him."

"Okay."

Shorty's quick response let me know she definitely wanted me to decline. I knew that Marcus would never like me anyway. For all I knew, he was also madly in love with Shorty, just like Reggie.

Shorty

I was so glad that Elida said she didn't want Marcus. I know I said I would just get over it, but I don't know if it would be that easy. If he and Elida got together, I don't know what I would do. Does that make me selfish? I mean, I do have a man. And it's not like I own Marcus or anything.

Janie just called my phone, out of the blue. I had been trying to stay in contact with her, but she barely answers her phone. She said she wanted to go somewhere, so I decided to go out and meet her.

We needed to catch up anyway.

"Hey, what's up?" said Janie. She looked kind of distant, not like herself.

"What's going on with you?"

"You ready to go?" She didn't answer my question, and that kind of raised a flag for me, but I decided not to press it.

"Where are we going?"

"To this guy's house. I want to get some money right quick."

I had a bad feeling about what she just said, but I agreed anyway. We walked to the house, which was a couple of blocks over. Janie knocked on the door, and an older, creepy looking man opened it.

"Hey. Is Lucas here?" said Janie.

The creepy guy smiled. "He's upstairs."

We entered the house, and I tried to stay close to Janie because I didn't know what the hell we might have just walked into. We went up the stairs to what I presumed to be Lucas' room, and Janie knocked. The door opened, and another older guy answered, this one even more creepy looking than the first guy! He looked like he was about 40 years old.

"Janie," he said, looking her up and down in a way that made me uncomfortable. Janie turned around to face me.

"Shorty, you can sit right here." She directed me to a seat that was in the hallway.

I reluctantly sat down, feeling more and more weird by the second.

Janie and Lucas went into the room and closed the door. I heard them in there talking and laughing for a few minutes, then I heard them turn on some music. They turned it up to a loud enough volume to where I couldn't hear what they were saying. That made me nervous, but I tried to play it off and started texting Reggie and Elida on my phone.

Janie and Lucas were in there for at least 20 minutes before I started to feel anxious. What were they doing in there? I got up from my seat to go knock on the door, and Lucas and Janie finally emerged.

"Time to go!" said Janie, looking a little too cheerful for my liking.

I wordlessly followed her back down the stairs because I wanted to get the hell out of that house. Once we got outside, I immediately started questioning her.

"Janie, what the hell was that? Who were those guys? Why were you in there so long?"

Janie looked at me like I was stupid. "Um, hello, I told you I needed some money." She pulled out a wad of bills from her front pocket. "He gave me two hundred dollars!"

She looked extremely excited.

"Janie, what did you do to get that money?" I couldn't believe what I was seeing or hearing.

"What the hell do you think?"

"Janie! That's sick!"

"Well, if I knew you were going to judge me, I would have never asked you to come," she huffed.

"That's not judgment. That's common sense! You could get hurt, or get a disease."

"No one can hurt me more than I've already been hurt."

I could see the lifelessness in her eyes. My heart panged. What was happening to my friend? I didn't even know what to do, or what to say to her.

"Janie, who hurt you," I finally managed.

"Don't worry about it."

"Were you raped?" I asked her, point blank.

She didn't respond. She didn't need to.

"We should go to the police!"

"For what?" she sucked her teeth. "I've slept with so many guys since then, all of his evidence is long gone. Besides, all he would have to say is that I wanted it, and it would be my word against his. A low life, trailer trash piece of scum against a poster boy for the city's biggest football team!"

"It's still not right." I felt defeated.

"Yeah, but life is not right. As long as I get my money, I'm good." Her tone and expression were devoid of emotion.

"Janie, you can't live like this."

"And why not?" she said, looking like she already knew what I was going to say.

"Because... you need to get help. What you're doing is dangerous. You're changing, and unfortunately, it's not for the better."

"Well, you changed too, dammit!" She yelled. "You changed too, Shorty. You're not like you used to be either. You talk different. You act different. You hang with different people... What? You think you're better than me now? Just because I'm not on the honor roll, that makes you more of a person than me? Well, you're not! You are no better than me!"

"I never said I was. You should see someone. You need help."

"Don't tell me what the hell I need. What I need for you is to stop judging me, and let me live my life. What's left of it."

She stalked off, leaving me standing there on the sidewalk.

Damn.

Elida

I'm sick of rejection. I've been thinking about all the past events in my life, and it seems like all I've faced is rejection. Rejection from my father, rejection from most of the girls at school until I met Shorty, and rejection from guys.

It's crazy how the four of us became such close friends, just to have both Reggie and Marcus fall for Shorty, and nobody fall for me.

Not that I wish anything bad against her, but damn.

Nobody?

I stared at myself in the mirror.

What could be wrong with me? Was I too fat? Were they all lying when they said I was pretty, when the whole time I was really ugly?

What was it?

My buzzing phone on my bed interrupted my thoughts.

I went to answer it, and it was Daddy of all people.

"Hey," I answered, not bothering to sound excited. It had been over six months since the last time we spoke.

"Well hello to you too. How are you and your brother and sister?"

"We're good, Daddy."

"Your mom still with that guy?"

Shawn had already moved in. He and my mother were planning to get married within the next few weeks. None of us kids wanted it to happen, but we had no say in the matter.

"Yup." I sighed.

"Hm. Well how about I come pick you guys up this weekend?"

"Sure."

"Are you okay?"

"Yes."

"Why are you only giving me one-word answers then?"

"I'm in the middle of doing homework."

"Oh, I'm sorry, Miss Smarty Pants." He chuckled like he believed me. *Pathetic.* "Well, I'll let you get back to your work. Tell Sammy to go get the house phone so I can talk to him and Gabriella."

"Okay."

We hung up.

"Sammy! Daddy's about to call!"

Shorty

I had just got in the house after a trip to the mall when my cell phone rang. It was Reggie. I smiled, then tapped 'Answer'. "Hello?" I said, trying to sound sexy, yet unbothered.

"Hey girl," said Reggie in this unrealistically deep voice.

I burst out laughing. "Boy, if you don't stop!"

"What?" he said, still using the voice. "You don't like Barry White?"

"Boy, bye. You do not sound like no Barry White!"

He burst out laughing too. "What you doing?" He switched back to his regular tone.

"Nothing, just got home from the mall."

"And you ain't invite me?" He faked like he was offended.

"Um, no. I don't get down with squares."

"Oh, it's like that?"

"Yup."

"So anyway, what else is new with you?"

"Nothing. I kind of been down lately."

His voice switched to concern. "Oh really? What about?"

"Janie."

"What's up with Janie?"

I explained to him what was going on, trying to paint her in the best light possible because she was still my friend, but at the same time, letting him know how worried I was.

"Damn. I knew she was out there, but not like that."

"Yeah. I don't know what to do."

"And her mom just doesn't care at all?"

I sighed. "It doesn't seem like it."

"Well... how about I come over and make you feel better?"

I sucked my teeth. I just poured out my heart to this boy, and he was trying to flirt! "Reggie, now is not the time for games!"

"Nah, Shorty, you misunderstood me. I meant like, do you want me to come over so we could talk about it face to face. I wasn't playing around."

I immediately felt guilty. "Oh, I'm sorry. I would have you come chill, but my mother is not home, and if you came and she saw you, she would trip."

"Oh, I understand."

"Can I come over your house instead?"

"Sure. You want me to come over there so I can walk you?"

"Nah, I got it."

"You sure? It's getting kind of late. I don't want anything to happen to you."

"I'll be fine, Reggie. But thanks though."

Reggie only lived like two buildings over, so I wasn't worried about going over there myself. I did think it was sweet that he was trying to be so protective though. When I got to his door, he opened it with a big smile on his face. I started cheesing too. Reggie must really like me. I felt so special being with him.

"Can I get you anything?" he asked.

"Nah, I'm straight," I said.

"You sure?"

"Mm hm."

"Well, alright. Let's talk."

"Your mom won't get mad for me being here so late?"

"She won't care. What's up with you?"

"I don't even know." I sighed. "It's just like... me and Janie have been friends our whole lives. I know it probably doesn't seem like we were that close because of all the times we fought, but we really are like sisters. Then when we got to high school, it seemed like we just started to drift apart. She started having sex and smoking weed and skipping school, and it seems like I'm going in the opposite direction. She let me get jumped, she doesn't answer my phone calls, and then whenever we do get together, she constantly accuses me of trying to be better than her. I don't know how to fix it." I paused and looked at him to make sure he was still listening.

"Wow," Reggie said.

"I mean, I guess she was right that I changed, but I'm not trying to change to be better than her. I'm just trying to better myself period."

Reggie had been sitting back, listening intently to my words the entire time. The more I stared at him, the more my attraction to him grew. How come I never realized he was so fine? He licked and bit his lips, then shifted his seat so he was leaning forward, his elbows on his knees. He turned to face me before he spoke.

"Well, my perspective on the situation is..."

He started to explain what he was thinking, but I was so caught up in his looks, I was barely paying attention. I began to notice more and more little things about him. Like... the length of his lashes. They were so long, and then his hazel eyes were like icing on the cake. His skin was so smooth, blemish free. I wanted to reach out and stroke his cheek. His arm muscles were clearly defined from working out and playing basketball. His lips looked so juicy, so kissable. Whenever he licked them, it made my heart drop.

"Shorty?"

He was calling my name, but I was so lost in his sexiness, I could barely hear him.

"Shorty!"

I finally snapped out of it. "Huh?" I said, feeling embarrassed.

"Girl, you look like you caught in a trance. I mean, I know I'm fine, but damn." His face and cockiness made me burst out laughing.

"Boy, ain't nobody worried about you." I playfully pushed his head. He grabbed my arms, his grip firm, but gentle. He looked in my eyes, and I was almost lost again.

"Oh yeah?" He chuckled.

I could feel myself getting hot all over. This boy was too much.

"Yeah. Ain't nobody worried about you." I repeated, trying to sound more convincing this time.

"Mm hm." He narrowed his eyes. "So anyway, since we pouring out our hearts and souls to each other, how about we make this thing official?"

"What do you mean?" He had caught me off guard switching the subject so quick.

"I want you to be my girl." He wasted no time. "I been wanting to be with you for a while, but I was too scared to say anything before. But I think you're really cool, and beautiful, and I don't want no other nigga to snatch you up before we could get together."

Everything he said was good until that last sentence. I gave him the side eye. "Really, Reggie?"

He chuckled. "Yeah, I really like you. It may not have came out the way I wanted, but I think you're cool people. I need somebody like you in my life."

My heart melted. "That was much better". I smiled, but then I turned serious. "Look, if we're really going to be together, I need you to know a few things."

"I'm listening."

"I'm not one of these girls that you are about to butter up and say nice things to, just so you can get in my pants. I'm a virgin, and I plan on staying that way until I find something real. You feel me?"

"I got you."

"So, if sex is what you're looking for, it's off the table. I'm letting you know that now."

He looked kind of surprised at my words.

"Why you looking at me like that?" I was starting to feel upset. Why was he looking so surprised? Did he think I was about to give it to him?

"Nothing. I just never really hear girls talk like you."

"What do you mean?"

"Like... you're so bold. You're not afraid to stand on your beliefs. I think that's sexy as hell."

I smiled, relieved. For a minute there, I thought I had Reggie pegged wrong, but he was showing me now that he was a good guy. My father had taught me well. I could hear his words echoing in my mind. "Don't be giving yourself to all these boys, Darlin'." He would say. "You ain't got to be stuck up about it, but stand your ground, and if he's really ready to be a man about it, he'll respect you. That's how you separate the grown men from the boys." I loved my father so much. I couldn't wait til he got out.

My eyes filled with tears at the thought of him.

"What's wrong?" said Reggie, immediately noticing my change in demeanor.

"Nothing." I tried to switch back to what we were talking about. "I appreciate you respecting my beliefs."

"No doubt. I mean, it will probably be hard, because I'm not a virgin, but I'll try my best."

"Who you been sleeping with?" I felt extremely jealous for some reason.

Reggie chuckled. "Girl, don't worry about that. It's not that many people though."

"People?" I wrinkled my nose. "So there were more than one?"

"Look, I ain't perfect."

"Nobody said you had to be."

"Anyway, the past is the past. This is about me and you now."

Reggie

Shorty was really one of a kind.
The more our conversation continued, the more I wanted her, though she literally just told me that sex wasn't an option.

Girls basically threw themselves at me. Ever since I made varsity, sex was never a problem. I ended up losing my virginity the first party me, Marcus, and Dave went to with Rex and them.

The older players saw it as an initiation to give us some girls to *get our feet wet*, as they called it. The girl I slept with, Tina, was a junior.

Marcus had this girl named Malika, a sophomore, and Dave had a girl named Bethany, a senior.

I couldn't front, I enjoyed every moment of it, and we were able to get more girls at all the other parties we went to during that year.

The whole time though, my feelings for Shorty kept growing and growing. Despite all the females

I was messing with at the parties, none of them could compare to her.

"Reggie?" Shorty said, shaking me from my thoughts. It was my turn to play it off.

"What? I heard you."

She crossed her arms. "Okay, what did I say then?"

I tried to keep a straight face. "You said... I'm the best boyfriend in the world."

She pushed my head. "Shush. We've only been together for five seconds."

I opened my mouth to say something else slick, but the key turned in the front door, and my mom walked in.

"Hey!" she said. "Shorty, how are you?"

"Hi!" Shorty said, then blushed. "I'm good."

She looked at me. "Did you do your homework?"

"I was about to."

"Great." She pursed her lips. "Well I guess you need to walk Shorty home then, so you can get started."

My mom was blocking like a muthafucka, but I wasn't about to start an argument.

"Okay. I'll be right back."

"See you later, Miss Tripp," Shorty said.

"You too. Tell your mom I said hi."

Shorty

Reggie walked me home, and I started doing my homework. As soon as he returned to his place, however, he facetimed me, so we goofed off for a couple more hours, then we actually did our homework together while we were still talking.

I was just drifting off to sleep when my mother burst into my room, banging the door against the wall. She flicked on the light. I jumped up, my heart pounding in fear.

"What's going on?" I asked, my eyes wide.

SMACK! My face instantly burned with pain.

"Who was that boy you were with?" Her voice boomed with accusation.

"Reggie."

"What were you doing with him? Why were you gone for so long?"

"Huh?"

"Don't play with me. Ronald saw you when you left to go to his house. I know his mother probably wasn't home. What were y'all doing?"

"We wasn't doing nothing, Ma. We were just talking."

She smacked me again.

"BULLSHIT!" She yanked my arm and snatched me out of bed. She shoved me into the hallway. "I am sick and tired of you lying to me!" She was pushing and punching me all the way toward the stairs.

"I'm not lying!" I was trying to say, but she was so full of rage, she didn't even notice I was talking. She shoved me really hard, and I lost my balance, falling down the stairs. I was holding onto the banister as I fell, so it cushioned my fall slightly, but I tumbled down pretty far before I finally got a good grip.

"Clean this house!" she yelled, then she went into her room and slammed the door.

I just sat there for a moment, my body filled with pain, clinging to the banister.

Elida

Shorty called and told me what her mom did to her. When she cried, I cried. It seemed like her situation was so hopeless. Every time something good happened to her, something bad would happen to ruin it. I was really feeling for my friend. She didn't even do anything wrong.

I went to my mom's room because I wanted to tell her what was going on, but I stopped short when I heard soft music playing.

I was about to knock, when I realized her bed was creaking.

I stepped back like I had just seen a venomous snake, almost bumping into Sammy.

He shot me a dirty look. "Watch where you're going."

"I didn't see you."

"Why were you going to Mommy's room?"

My face reddened. "I wanted to tell her something but…"

"Yeah, I know," he said. "They think they're quiet in there, but I always hear them."

Sammy's room was the closest to my mom's.

"Ew!" I said.

"I know, but what are we going to do about it? Not like Daddy's coming back." Sammy's voice was so cold when he said that, I wanted to hug him.

"Sammy, Daddy makes his own decisions, just like Mommy. At least Shawn is cool."

Sammy stepped back like I wounded him. "Cool? You're turning against Daddy?"

"No, but..."

"But what?"

"Nothing. I'm just going to go back to my room."

"Fine."

On my way back to my room, I peeked in at Gabriella. She was fast asleep.

It was after eleven. I needed to head to bed too, if I wanted to wake up on time in the morning.

Shorty

I was sore for a while after my mother beating me and pushing me down the stairs. I walked with a slight limp at school the next day. I hurt physically, but the emotional pain was worse. It's like she didn't even care about me. I could have hit my head and died.

Thank God I held onto the banister.

I went to my first class and put my head down on my desk. I had a crazy headache and just wanted the day to be over. I could feel my throat tightening up as my tears fell. I was trying to hold on, but life was just too overwhelming.

"Shorty?" I heard Reggie's voice, but I didn't want to be bothered.

"Leave me alone!" My voice was muffled as I spoke.

"What's wrong, baby?" His voice was so tender, I had to look up.

"Nothing!" I felt like I was losing control.

He sat down next to me, full of concern. "I brought you some juice." He placed it in front of me. My heart was so full, I burst into tears. How could he be so sweet to me? He put his arm around me and tried to soothe me.

"It's gonna be okay." Reggie tried to speak in a low voice so people wouldn't be all in my business. It was hard to do though, because people were starting to come in, and they were all staring at me, wondering why I was crying. "What happened?" He whispered.

"We'll have to talk later," I whispered back.

He nodded in understanding and continued to rub my shoulder. He helped me calm down, and we started to drink our juice, trying to hurry up and finish before the teacher came and made us throw it away.

Reggie

I worried about Shorty all day. We didn't get to talk much during the three classes we shared with each other, but then I was gonna have practice after school.

I couldn't be late, but I was determined to see what was up with her.

After my last class, I raced to her locker.

I had sent her a text saying I was meeting her there. I hoped she was able to get there on time because I only had twenty minutes to get changed and get to the gym.

I arrived there just before she did.

"Hey," she said when she approached.

"Hey." I bent down and kissed her cheek.

She blushed, though I could tell she was still hurting.

"What happened?" I spoke in a low voice.

She stared up at me. "Reggie, my mom keeps hitting me."

"Hitting you? You mean like a whooping?"

A dark expression crossed her features. "It's more than a whooping."

I listened in shock, then anger, then hurt and disappointment as Shorty told me how her mom had been physically abusing her since freshman year. I knew she had hit her that one time, but I didn't know it was ongoing. My heart was all twisted up hearing that. My mind raced with different options.

I almost said, "What about your dad?" but then I remembered Shorty's dad was locked up.

I hated to see her trapped like this.

"Shorty, I'm skipping practice," I told her. "We can go to my house, then maybe we can talk to my mom about what to do."

She looked afraid. "No, Reggie. You can't miss practice."

"I can for you."

She shook her head more adamantly. "No. I'm not having you get in trouble with your coach over me. I'll figure it out."

I grabbed her hand. "We can figure it out together."

"Reggie, please just go to practice. We can talk when you get home."

I felt like I was caught between a rock and a hard place. I knew I had to go to practice, but at the same time, I didn't want to leave her like that. "You sure?"

Just then, Rex was rushing down the hall.

"Reg, what the fuck you doing? Practice is in five minutes!"

"Go," Shorty urged.

I didn't want to leave her, but I felt like I had no choice. I kissed her forehead. "I'm gonna call you as soon as I get home. Please pick up."

"Okay."

I ran after Rex down the hallway, but I looked back at Shorty one more time before I entered the locker room.

Shorty

I took the bus home after school, feeling numb.
 I didn't even want to go home. My mind went to my Auntie Gina. Maybe she would let me stay with her? I thought about it for a few moments, then my phone buzzed with a call.

It was my dad's correctional facility.

I accepted the call. "Hello? Daddy?"

"Hey Darlin'!" Daddy said.

I didn't know how he did it, but whenever I heard Daddy's voice, it made me feel at ease.

"How are you?" I asked.

"Keeping my nose clean. How's school?"

"School is good. I'm passing all my homework assignments so far."

"Look at my sweet girl. I knew you could do it."

"Thank you."

"Is something bothering you, Darlin'?"

I was surprised that he could pick up my tone, but I tried to fix it. "No, I'm good. I just have a headache." I didn't want to tell Daddy what was going on with Ma, one because there was nothing he could do about it being locked up, and for two because I didn't want him worried.

If his mind was amped up about me, he could end up getting in trouble. I wanted him out of that place, not to have to stay longer for fighting or something.

I got off the phone with my father just as the bus hit my spot.

I exited and made my way toward my Auntie's house. At least it was worth a try. I knocked on her door, not sure what I was going to say.

She opened it before I had a chance to think.

"Hey!" she said, looking surprised.

"Auntie, can I come in?"

"You can for a second. I was about to leave."

I entered, and she closed the door.

"What's up with you?" she asked.

I decided to just come out with it. "Auntie, I was wondering if I could come stay with you for a while."

Her head snapped back. "Stay with me for a while? Did your mother kick you out?"

"No, but... I want to leave."

"Alize... I'm not about to have you coming to my house causing trouble."

I blinked. "Causing trouble?"

"I know about you. You are out there fighting and doing all kinds of things. Your mother tells me."

"Auntie Gina, I haven't had a fight since last year. I've been doing good in school. I just need..."

My voice trailed off as I saw it was no use. My aunt was a brick wall.

Elida

Me and Marcus shared one class together that Reggie and Shorty weren't in. I walked in and sat next to him. He turned to me. "Hey, do you feel weird now?"

I paused. "Weird how?"

"Now that Shorty and Reggie are together."

Now that he had said it, I wasn't sure how to respond. I hoped he wasn't about to confess to me his feelings for her, because that would hurt so bad.

My crush on Marcus had only grown since freshman year. I couldn't help it. Marcus was cool, sweet, sexy... I could go on and on.

But I couldn't do shit about it if he was feeling Shorty.

I shrugged. "Not really. They seem to be happy though."

Marcus chuckled. "Right. He gets all googly eyed when she's around now."

I opened my notebook as the teacher walked in.

"Did you do your homework?" Marcus asked.

I nodded. "Did you?"

"Yeah."

Mr. Simpson started the lesson, and we had to stop our conversation. Throughout the class, however, I kept wondering why Marcus was asking me about Shorty and Reggie. Was he jealous? Maybe he had a long-term crush on her too, and now Reggie stole his chance.

I wanted to know, but I didn't want to ask.

Marcus

When I got home from school, Dad was sitting at the kitchen table, eating some Corn Flakes.

"Isn't it a little late for breakfast?" I joked.

I warmed up some pasta from the night before.

"I just had a taste for it," he replied.

I sat across from him when my food was done heating.

"Son, I don't get to tell you this enough, but I'm proud of how you're turning out."

I looked up at Dad from my food. "Thanks."

"How are things with the team?"

"We're good. We have a game coming up in a couple of weeks."

"I'll definitely be there. I'm so mad I missed your first season being deployed."

"It's not like I got a lot of playing time anyway."

"Still, I wanted to be there."

"I understand you have work."

"Marcus."

His one word halted me.

"I know that things have been tough since me and your mother split, but I don't want you staying in a negative mind state about it. You're doing good academically and with sports, but I don't want you feeling any type of way due to our situation."

I was shocked that Dad picked up on my mood, when I tried so hard to hide it. "She went and married that dude, Dad."

"I understand that, and it hurt me too, but I'm getting over it. I found someone new myself."

My ears grew hot. "What? Who?"

"She's a marine, like me." From the expression on my dad's face when he spoke about her, I could tell he was serious about this mystery woman.

"You never mentioned meeting anybody before."

"It wasn't the time. But I'm telling you now, because I need you to forgive your mother, Son. What happened between me and her affected you, no doubt. But you can't live the rest of your life holding a grudge."

Shorty

Janie was never pregnant. I am so heated, I can't even think straight. This chick lied, catfished some dude using my name, and got me jumped by Shaneeda and her friends, all for no reason.

I really don't even know what to think anymore. Janie and I were friends for so long, I can't even understand how she would do something like this to me. Of course, we had our fights. But we always made up though. I never crossed her in this way, and I don't understand why she would do it to me.

Even with what happened to her, there is no excuse. So what? Somebody hurt you, so you take it out on me? How is that fair?

The way that I found out was that I bumped into Shaneeda's man while I was at the mall. I didn't even know it was him at first, because I never seen him before, but we were talking about people at the school, and he got around to saying he was dating Shaneeda. I asked him for how long, and he said they had been dating for over a year. That's how I knew he was the same guy that she jumped me for.

When I told him my name was Shorty, he looked so surprised.

I didn't tell him about how his girlfriend jumped me, but I did ask him about Janie. That's when he said that he and Janie never actually slept together – she just topped him off a few times!

When I heard that, I was so heated. So this bitch was never pregnant in the first place! I can't believe this girl. I'm more hurt than anything. I really just don't understand. On the one hand, I feel like I should confront her, but on the other hand, I don't even see the point. Janie is out there doing God knows what. She probably won't even take the conversation seriously, and that would piss me off, and then we would be fighting. I don't have the time.

Another 'bombshell' – I think Marcus likes Elida.

It seems like every time we talk about her when we are alone, or when all of us are together, he has this look in his eye. I don't know how to take that. Even though I'm clearly with Reggie, I've been crushing on Marcus for years! If he and Elida got together, I don't know what I would do. I don't want to be selfish, but still!

My phone rang, shaking me from my thoughts. Low and behold, it was Reggie. "Hello?" I said.

"Hey, Shorty!" I could practically see his dimples through the phone.

"What's up."

"What's wrong with you? Did something new happen with your mom?"

"No, but I found out some bullshit about Janie."

I told him what Shaneeda's boyfriend told me.

"Wow..." he said when I finished. "You gonna have to let that girl go, Shorty."

"I know, but it's hard. We've been friends our whole lives."

"Same with me and Dave and E, so I understand."

"Y'all are not friends no more?" I was becoming confused.

"We still cool for now, but I feel like shit is getting worse and worse." He told me the latest. E was fully immersed in the RECKLESS gang with this older guy Nino and his crew, and Dave was trying to get down too.

"I keep telling him, Dave, you don't want to go that route. But he got it in his mind that me and Marcus are lames."

"Wow..." I was speechless. Who knew something as simple as going to high school and wanting to better yourself would bring all this?

"Anyway, did you want to hang out today?"

"Today?" I repeated.

"Yeah, I figured we could hit up a movie or something."

"Um..."

"Um, what?"

"Me and Marcus were supposed to hang out today."

"What were you going somewhere with him for?" Reggie sounded confused.

"Well, Elida's going too."

"But you didn't mention her at first. You only named Marcus. Plus Marcus never said shit to me. Why are y'all three going somewhere, and I wasn't invited?"

Reggie sounded confused, and his confusion confused me.

"Chill, Reggie. We made plans to hang out; that's all."

"So you're telling me that you are not going to go nowhere with me, your man, because you trying to hang out with my boy?" He sounded like he was going from zero to one hundred. I tried to pump his brakes.

"Reggie, stop jumping to conclusions."

"I'm not jumping to conclusions, Shorty! Explain to me why my girl don't wanna spend time with me, but she want to spend time with my boy!"

"Reggie..."

"What?"

"Calm down."

"What you mean, calm down? You making me feel like you want him over me or something."

"You're making this deeper than what it should be. Me and Marcus always hang out. We chilled together before me and you even got together."

"Yeah, but all that shit should change now that I'm your man."

"Oh, so now you're running my life?"

"Don't put words in my mouth. You know what I meant. How would you feel if I dissed you 'cause I was hanging with some other chick?"

"Reggie, nobody is dissing you. I have no problem hanging out with you."

"But not if you already had plans with Marcus."

"Reggie, it's not even like that."

CLICK. He hung up on me. That immediately got me heated. *How dare he?* I quickly called him back.

"Hello?" he said roughly.

"Who do you think you hanging up on?"

"You. You acting like you don't give a fuck about me, so I hung up."

"It wasn't even like that."

"Yes it was."

"Why do you have such an attitude?"

"Whatever, man. You done running your mouth?"

"Reggie, you talking crazy right now!"

"Are you done?"

"You know what?" I stared at the phone. "I'm trying to have a conversation with you, but if this is how you are going to act, *I'm* done." He had definitely just hurt my feelings. I went to click the End button.

"Wait." His attitude changed.

"What? What do you want now?"

"I'm sorry, Baby. I overreacted."

I rolled my eyes, but smiled as I calmed. "Oh, now you sorry?"

"Yeah. I didn't mean to talk to you like that."

"Well... don't let it happen again."

After I got off the phone with Reggie, Marcus called. I talked to him for a second, but I told him I had to cancel our plans because I ended up making new plans with Reggie. He didn't even sound disappointed! He just said that it was cool and that he and Elida would still go.

"Matter of fact, I just realized I never told Reggie we were hanging out!" Marcus said. "My bad."

"I didn't tell him either."

I didn't go into how Reggie blew up at me about it, because I didn't want to cause any drama in their friendship.

"I guess the four of us can get up another time. Let me call Elida."

He hung up before I could say anything else.

Wow. I feel like my suspicions are being confirmed. If Marcus likes Elida, and Elida already told me how she felt about him, it's only a matter of time before they get together! I don't know what I'm going to do. I know it's selfish to be with one boy and still try to hold onto another, especially when it comes to your best friend, but this was just too much.

Reggie

I feel like I'm trippin.
    At the same time, I think I'm seeing some shit that I don't want to see. I think Shorty likes Marcus. I picked up on it a couple of weeks ago when we were all hanging out, and I noticed that her jokes were more like flirts in his direction.
    Marcus didn't respond to it. I don't even think he noticed, but I did.
    I feel like I'm in a fucked up position, but I'm gonna just try to ride it out.
    Maybe I'm misunderstanding.
    Shorty did cancel her plans with Marcus and Elida to chill with me, and Marcus just texted me saying him and Elida were hitting up the mall. He asked if me and Shorty was down, but I said no.
    I just need some time to process this shit.

Elida

I was walking out of a convenience store near my house when this fine ass nigga stopped me.

"Yo, Mami. Hold on."

He gave me a seductive look. I immediately started to feel nervous. I had never had this happen to me before in my life. "Are you talking to me?" I asked, immediately feeling stupid afterward. Of course, he was talking to me!

"Yeah." He smiled.

"What's going on?" I tried to sound relaxed, like this happened all the time.

"What's up with you?" He licked his lips. I felt a little shiver. He was making me nervous again. What was I supposed to say? How was I supposed to respond?

"Um, nothing." *Could you be more awkward, Elida?* My thoughts screamed at me. Here was my one chance to actually talk to a guy who seemed like he was interested, and I was totally blowing it!

"You got a man?"

My heart dropped. "Um, no." *Stop saying 'Um'!* "You looking for one?"

Oh, my Gosh! What am I supposed to say? My heart started racing. I opened my mouth to answer, but then the guy burst out laughing. Two other boys came from around the corner, laughing too. One of them gave him some dap.

I felt a burning sensation all over my body, starting at my heart. What was this? Why were they laughing?

"You did that, nigga?" said one of his friends.

"Yeah," said the guy who spoke to me, still beside himself with laughter. "She thought I was tryina holla!"

He had his hands on his stomach, doubled over, laughing.

I felt so humiliated. I pushed past him and his friends and ran back to my house. When I got there, I ran upstairs to my room and slammed the door. I plopped down on my bed, the tears streaming down my cheeks. *Why doesn't anybody like me? Why did it have to be a joke?*

I stared down at my hands, my eyes blurry from the tears. They were trembling. I sniffled.

Just then, my door opened and Sammy walked in. "Elida."

"What are you doing? Get out of my room!"

Gabriella heard us and came in too. "Elida, why are you crying?"

"I'm not crying! Shut up and get out!" Gabriella turned and went back to her room.

"You leave too," I said to Sammy.

"What are you going to do if I don't?"

"Get out, Sammy!"

"I feel like staying here."

"Sammy, get out and leave me alone!"

He walked over and hopped on my bed. "Nope."

"Sammy, I'm not in the mood."

"Ooh, I'm real scared now. I think I'm gonna run away."

"You're not funny. Get out and leave me alone."

"Why are you so mad? Did Marcus diss you?"

"GET OUT!" I screamed at the top of my lungs. He got up and went toward the door like he was leaving, then turned back. He reached down into my dirty clothes basket, and he threw a balled-up sock at me. Then another one.

I jumped up out of the bed and punched him in the face.

"OW, YOU bitch!" He shouted. We were lucky Mommy was out with Shawn. He tried to hit me back, but I grabbed his arm and flung him out the door, slamming it behind him.

"MUTHAFUCKA!" I heard him yell, then I heard his feet thundering down the stairs.

Shorty

I walked into my Geometry class kind of late because I went to the bathroom first. We had a sub. He was just sitting there with a blank expression on his face, listening to music and drumming his fingers on the desk. I walked up to him and he pulled off his headphones.

"Sign the attendance." He handed me a piece of paper and put his headphones back on. I went to my seat. I noticed the entire class was silent.

"What's everybody all quiet for?"

"'Cause Dave and E are about to battle," Reggie replied. The seats were rearranged in sort of a circle, with Dave and E standing in the middle. "Come sit next to me." Reggie gestured toward an empty seat. I obliged. "What, I can't get a hug or nothing?"

I rolled my eyes, gave him a hug, and kissed his cheek.

"That's better," he smirked.

"Yo, eyo eyo eyo…" E began. I rolled my eyes again. I could tell that whatever bars he was about to spit were useless.

"Are you gonna start, or what?" Dave said, clearly ready to go all out.

"Shut up," E responded, becoming cockier by the second.

"I said… I'm boutta rip this mic, you gonna be sorry aight?

Look at all these hoes on the street, Imma straight pimp cuz they be licking my feet

A bullet from my oozie come to ya head like heat

My flow is so sick you don't even deserve me

Put you in my mouth eat you up like a Hershey!"

E made a 'mic drop' signal, then raised both his hands upward and backward like he just did something great.

Dave just laughed. "Nigga, that was trash!"

"I give him about 3 bars," said Reggie.

"I give him two and a half," said Marcus.

E sucked his teeth. "Man, fuck both of y'all. Dave, what you got?" He stared at Dave expectantly.

"Aight, aight," Dave responded. He looked at a girl who was sitting to the side of him. "Watch this." He winked at her. "I'm about to end this dude. Check it…

I give it to you raw, butt naked

> *Come up on my block and it's gonna get hectic*
> *When I kill ya moms you ain't gonna expect it*
> *Then Imma sit in the shade underneath my hammock*
> *And eat a sandwich."*

When Dave was finished, you could practically hear a pin drop. The entire classroom had the same *WTF??* expression on their faces.

A boy named Ron jumped in the battle, entering the center of the circle where Dave and E stood. "Yo, I'm bout to save ya life, Dave." He nudged Dave playfully.

> *"I'm bout to bring out this gangsta shit*
> *You must not know what you talkin bout*
> *I'll pop my trunk like I come from down south*
> *Imma kill you then kill myself*
> *So I'll be able to slap ya spirits*
> *Leave ya body spiritless*
> *Have ya parents delirious*
> *My whole flow is serious."*

Ron stepped back triumphantly. E licked his lips, clearly intimidated. "A'ight, a'ight. You might have a little something." He looked at Dave, but Dave sat down. "I guess I got this then." He licked his lips again, then he got his inspiration.

> *"I said... My flow goes more like blow for blow*
> *I never get old, my rhymes will never get cold*
> *I'm better than most, once you find out I'm better you ghost*

Not meaning to boast, but we all know E is the truest
Spit fire in my bars and my beats is the fluid
Nigga get to it, don't hate 'cause you know I'm the best
My flow is like a bullet have you sportin a vest."

"OOOOOOHHHHH!!" The class erupted in applause. Most were impressed with E's bars. I had to give it to him – he was pretty good that time. I looked over at the substitute to see if he was even still there. He appeared to be completely oblivious to the scene before him.

He had his legs propped up on the desk, his head laid back, and his eyes closed, zoning out to the music in his headphones. He was way more chill than most subs we had, but I wasn't going to complain. I didn't feel like doing any schoolwork anyway.

"I got next," said Shaniqua, the girl who Dave had winked at earlier.

"Next?" E blinked at her.

She stood up and entered the center of the circle. "Yeah, nigga. You got a problem? Or you scared a female gonna beat you?"

"OOOOOHHHH!" The class was even more riled up now. I knew Shaniqua had bars. She already had a mixtape out and had even done a music video.

"I don't do that commercial shit," said E. "Straight bars only."

She shrugged. "Okay." She drew out the word.

"I'll go first," said E. He turned to his boys, Reggie, Marcus, and Dave.

"Yall got this chick thinking she could possibly be better than dudes
I don't mean to, but I'mma have to be rude
This chick think she could win against a nigga like me?
Please Ma, go home and play wit your barbies
I'm sorry for hurting you and sounding real greasy
But when it comes to the big leagues, it ain't gonna be easy."

A few people clapped after E's verse.

"Weak," Shaniqua responded, not looking the least bit intimidated.

E opened his mouth to say something back, but she was already going in.

"This battle with you is a waste of time
No bars, you wack, so this is a waste of rhyme
You wish you was me but you ain't built with the wit
I'll lay your ass out, make your fat ass fit
I ain't no bitch, leave your stupid ass in a ditch
I make the switch, leave your fuckin face in a stitch."

"OOOOOHHHHH!" The class erupted in applause.

Shaniqua was in her zone. "Hold up! I wasn't finished." She continued.

*"Even though we ain't matched physically
My glock spray'll set you straight quite simply
Give up before I put you out your misery
You can't win against me, it's not meant to be."*

When Shaniqua's verse ended, E looked embarrassed.

Reggie jumped up and down in excitement. "She killed you, son!" He shouted at E, giving Shaniqua a high five and a bear hug. Everyone in the class was clapping.

Even the substitute, who had taken off his headphones during Shaniqua's verse, looked impressed. Anybody with eyes could tell that E wanted to crawl under a table.

"She did not win, yo." He looked back and forth between his boys and the rest of the class.

"She got you, son," Marcus said, shaking his head.

"Man, bullshit. Bar for bar? You serious, nigga?" I could practically see steam coming from E's ears.

"Don't be a sore loser," Shaniqua said with a smirk, then she picked up her backpack as the bell rang. Everyone began pushing the desks back to their original places. Outside, the hallway was abuzz with students going back and forth about who they thought won the battle.

Elida

E was stewing next period over the fact that people said he lost the battle to a girl. For me, that's kind of an eye roll. I mean, to be mad just because you lost to a girl seems pretty weak to me. Society has progressed so much that it shouldn't matter.

Women are able to do a lot of things men can do, and some things, even better.

E didn't seem to get the memo though.

"Yo, watch where you going," E barked at Marcus. Marcus had accidentally tripped over E's foot as he was walking by him.

Marcus sucked his teeth. "It was an accident."

"Yo, who you think you talking to?" E stood up, way more upset than the situation called for.

"Bruh, you still salty? Just get over it. You win some, you lose some."

"Fuck you. You know that bitch ain't beat me."

Marcus held up his hands. "Hey man, that's not what our classmates say."

By now, everyone's eyes were on E and Marcus. We could all see that it was about to go down. Our teacher, Miss Perkins, finally arrived, and not a moment too soon.

"Hello everyone! Ready to get started?" She looked around the room, then her eyes settled on Marcus and E. "What's going on?"

"Nothing," Marcus quickly replied. "I was just going to sharpen my pencil." He held it up for emphasis.

"Pussy ass," E said under his breath, but loud enough for Marcus to hear.

Marcus turned back to face him. "What did you just say?"

"You heard me."

"Look E. We boys and everything, but you really need to calm down."

"Boys?" E looked at Marcus like he wanted to spit. "We ain't fuckin boys. You a fuckin lame. Always have been."

"Gentlemen, let's calm down," said Miss Perkins as she made her way over to where Marcus and E faced each other.

"Fuck this nigga," said E.

Reggie jumped up at that. "Chill, E. Where is this even coming from?"

Marcus continued, still upset. "Stop trying to bully me, E. I'm not a punk."

"Prove it," E countered.

"Why don't y'all just squash this?" said Reggie.

"Gentlemen, do I need to call security?" said Miss Perkins.

"Shut up, bitch!" said E.

"Watch your mouth, nigga! That's a teacher!" Marcus looked agitated.

"Fuck you gonna do about it?"

"That's it. I'm calling security!" said Miss Perkins, her face red from E calling her a bitch.

As soon as Miss Perkins turned to go toward the door, E lunged at her, but Marcus blocked him, socking E in the jaw.

"That's a woman!" he yelled.

E held his jaw for a second, then rushed Marcus.

They flipped over some desks, then quickly became engaged in an all out brawl. A few girls screamed. Some other students pulled out their phones to record. I moved out of the way in shock. I had never seen Marcus this mad before.

Poor Miss Perkins was on the phone with security, and they must have been right near our classroom, because they came running in to break them up.

Reggie helped the two guards as they pulled Marcus and E apart.

Then, E tried to swing on the guard that was holding him back and the guard slammed him to the ground, twisting his arms behind his back and cuffing him.

"This is crazy!" I said, taking in the scene.

"I'll fucking kill you!" E shouted at Marcus. "You're dead!"

Both Marcus and E were taken out of the classroom. After that, Miss Perkins seemed a little shaken up for the rest of the class as she tried to restore order and collect herself.

Reggie

Shit hit the fan today.
Marcus got suspended from school for a week, and suspended from practice for the next three weeks. His dad looked pissed when he came to pick him up.

I tried to call his phone a few times, but he didn't answer.

I caught back up with Dave while we were in the locker room before practice that day. "Yo Dave, what the fuck is wrong with E?"

Dave looked confused. "E? You mean, what the fuck is wrong with Marcus."

"Marcus didn't do shit wrong. I saw the whole thing."

"He knew E was a sore loser. He should have left it alone instead of saying that girl won the battle."

"E needs to stop acting like a little kid."

"Marcus needs to stop acting like a bitch."

We were standing toe to toe without even realizing it, when Rex and Coach got between us.

"Cool it off, you two," Coach said. "Marcus is suspended from practice for the next three weeks, but you need to keep your bullshit off the court."

Me and Dave stared at each other.

"Now shake like men."

Me and Dave shook hands like he said, but I could tell the shit that was brewing between us was far from over.

Marcus

My dad didn't say a word to me the whole way home, but when we pulled up to the complex, I saw my mom's car in the parking lot.

"Shit!" I said under my breath.

"Watch your fucking mouth!" Dad barked.

We walked into the apartment, where my mom had already let herself in.

"Marcus, what were you doing fighting?" My mom said when I walked in.

"Answer her!" My dad said, when he saw that I didn't respond.

"It wasn't my fault."

"How wasn't it your fault? What happened, Marcus?"

"Look, just leave me alone." I tried to push past her, but my dad gripped my arm and wrenched me back.

He gave me a menacing look and I immediately stopped struggling.

"You been disrespecting your mother for far too long. That shit stops today. You hear me?" He jacked me up a little further.

"Yes," I said.

He let me go.

"Now what happened?" My mother repeated.

I told them about the fight.

"Stay away from that kid E," my father said. "I never liked him, but I was trying to let you make your own decisions."

"I know, Dad. We're not even cool like that anymore."

"Marcus, how about you come and stay with me and Felix for a while? Just until things cool down with E?"

"No!" There was way too much bass in my voice when I spoke, but I calmed down when I saw the look my dad gave me. "I'm not gonna let him run me away from a neighborhood I grew up in, Mom."

"But the report said he threatened you, Marcus."

"E's not gonna do nothing."

"You can never be sure."

We stared at each other.

"How about we give it some time?" Dad interjected. "If the situation gets worse, you stay with your mother for a while. If everything dies down, you can stay here."

Shorty

A couple of weeks had passed since Marcus and E's fight. Reggie and Marcus steered clear of E, and they mostly only talked to Dave during practice due to the fact that Dave took E's side.

In my opinion, the whole thing was childish. E needed to grow up.

Me and Reggie were walking hand in hand around the park on a Saturday.

"Hey Shorty," he said with a half smile. "Can I ask you a question?"

"What?" I smiled back.

He stopped walking and turned so that he was facing me. He cocked his head to the side, his smirk still evident. "On a scale from one to ten, how much do you like me right now?"

"How much do I like you?"

"Yeah. How much?"

"Hmmm... Let me think." I stared into his eyes. "On a scale from one to ten?"

He nodded, staring back expectantly.

"I'd have to say... a four."

His expression shifted slightly, then his cocky grin returned. "A four, huh?"

"Yup."

"Oh, well uh..." He stepped even closer to me, so that I could smell his sexy cologne. His lips looked juicy as hell. Then he licked them.

I felt myself swoon.

"How we gonna fix that?" He put his arms around my waist. I put mine around his shoulders.

"I'm not sure. What do you have in mind?" I stared up into his sexy eyes, but before I could utter another word, his lips covered mine in a passionate kiss. *Whoowee! Reggie!*

Reggie

I can't front, Shorty got me open.
Being around her made me feel better about the way life was going.

I was still pissed about how everything went down with E. A lifelong friendship down the drain, but if that was what he wanted, so be it.

Dave chilled out after our argument. I don't know if he did it because he wants to try out for varsity in junior year, or because he really saw that he was trippin.

Either way, I have no choice but to keep my eyes open.

Marcus' dad put him on strict punishment after the fight until his suspension from the team ended, so he couldn't use his phone or nothing. In practice, he was allowed to sit on the bleachers and watch us, but Coach warned him not to even think of touching a basketball.

I felt for him, because neither of us knew if he would get any playing time for the rest of the season. Marcus wanted to try out for varsity next year too.

    Him and Dave both tried out at the beginning of this year, but Coach said they weren't ready.

Elida

I had just finished eating dinner with Mommy, Shawn, Gabriella, and Sammy. Sammy seemed to be warming up slightly to Shawn, though he clearly still wanted to hate him. I wanted to hate him too, but seeing that he was cool and made my mom happy kind of put me at ease.

Especially since Daddy seemed to not care what went on with us.

Gabriella had already completely accepted him, as soon as he brought her a new tablet to replace the old one she broke. Sammy was pissed that she turned so quickly, but Shawn brought him a cell phone, so he didn't complain too much.

My phone rang as soon as I went to my room. "Hello?" I answered.

"Girl, what's up?" said Shorty.

"I have to tell you something." From the tone of her voice, it sounded like it was going to be good.

"Ohh, spill the beans! What is it? Wait, I have to tell you something too!" I sat down on my bed, anticipating her response, also nervous about how she would take my news.

"Wait, what you gotta tell me?" she demanded.

"It's about this boy."

"What boy? What's his name?"

"Girl, you started it." I chuckled. "You go first."

"So... Me and Reggie were walking through the park, right."

"Mm hm?"

"He was like, 'Can I ask you a question?' and I was like 'What?' He was like, standing across from me while he was talking, so he was looking sexy as hell! Whoo, girl! So anyway, he said, 'How much do you like me?'"

I wrinkled my nose. "How much do you like him?"

"Yeah. On a scale from one to ten. So I told him I would give it a four. And he said we were going to have to fix that. I asked him how we were gonna fix it, and he kissed me!"

"Aw, sooky sooky! Was it good?"

"Hell yeah, it was good! That boy was working that tongue!"

"Damn, girl. I'm happy for you. I need somebody to kiss."

"What about you?" She switched gears. "What happened with this boy, Miss Thang?"

"Well, do you know a boy named Dayvaun?"

"Um... no, I don't think so. Who is that?"

"He hangs with Darnell and them." I said, referring to some guys at our school. "He's light skinned, sexy lips, curly hair, you know…"

"He sounds familiar, but I can't place him. Anyways, what happened?"

"I was at the mall, and –"

"Without me? Excuse me!" Shorty feigned like she was hurt.

"Girl, don't try it. You go to the mall without me all the time."

"Only to try to fill out applications. My savings are getting low ever since I left Unique Amusements when the season ended."

"I know that's right." I was proud of my friend for getting her first job. "I can't wait til we turn sixteen. Then we could really start working." Shorty's birthday was right before the end of the school year, and mine was right before the beginning.

"Agreed. But next time you go to the mall, definitely invite me."

"I will, but you were with Reggie this time anyway."

"True. What happened?"

"Like I said, I was at the mall. Dayvaun just came up to me out of nowhere and asked for my number. He told me he was going to call me, but I didn't believe him. Then when I got home, he called! We talked for like, mad long. It was hours. He seemed really cool. He said he liked me and wants us to start talking."

"Ooohhh, get it girl! Now we gotta set up some double dates! I need to meet this Dayvaun."

Marcus

I felt like it was not fair for me to have to sit out of whole games over a fight that wasn't my fault. I understood what Coach meant when he said that discipline was part of work ethic, but E started that shit.

I sat on the bench, mad as hell, my eyes scanning the crowd.

My mom and dad were both here to support. What, I didn't know, because I wasn't playing anyway. I was just about to focus back on the game when I spotted E, standing with Nino and his crew.

I tensed up immediately.

E didn't seem to notice me. He was focused on the game.

I looked over at Dave, who was also seated on the bench.

Dave had been acting real funny ever since the fight. He was currently seated a couple of players away from me, when we usually sat next to each other.

I wondered what that was about, since he claimed we were cool.

Reggie

We fought hard for the win but ended up losing.

I dropped 20 points, and Rex dropped 23, but that still didn't bring us the victory. The other school's team just fought harder, I guess.

Even though I was pissed, I tried not to get too mad about it. We were still in the running for the championship.

When we got to the locker room, however, Coach screamed on us.

"What the fuck were you doing out there? Huh?!" He stalked over to me and Rex. "Both of you could have pushed harder."

"Sorry, Coach," Rex said.

"I don't want to hear sorry. I want your ass in gear. We're too close to the championship for you guys to be fucking up now."

"Understood," I said.

Dave approached me and Marcus as we were headed to Marcus' dad's car. My mom had to work late tonight, so she couldn't make the game.

"Where y'all about to go?" he asked.

"Home. Where are you going?"

"I was about to get up with E and them."

"Dave..."

He tensed up. "What?"

"Just be careful out there, man."

"What the fuck is that supposed to mean?"

I wasn't about to get into it with him tonight. "Nothing man. See you later."

Shorty

Me and Elida were sitting in my kitchen. My mom and Ronald were both still at work, thank God.

"So, what did you and Dayvaun talk about yesterday?"

Elida and Dayvaun had been talking for a few weeks. They were so cute together. It seemed like things were finally starting to work out for Elida – she was getting a man and everything!

"He is soooo sweet! He always tells me that I'm pretty and stuff. He makes me feel beautiful." She hugged herself.

"Awww." I was happy for my friend.

Just then, we heard a knock on my front door. I went to answer it, and it was Marcus.

"Hey," he said, and gave me a hug before we made our way to the kitchen where Elida was still sitting.

"Hey, Marcus!" she shot him a bright smile.

He gave her a nervous smile. "Hey, how you been?"

"Elida and I were just talking about her little boyfriend." I teased Elida, causing her to blush.

Marcus flinched slightly. "Boyfriend? What boyfriend?" He sat down.

"Dayvaun. You know, the boy she's been talking to!" I swear, Marcus acts like he lives under a rock sometimes. He definitely knows about Dayvaun.

"So y'all go out now?" He looked pissed.

"No, not yet," Elida said, looking from me to Marcus. "Why are you trippin?"

"I'm not."

We continued our conversation, and I kept noticing that every few minutes or so, Marcus would sneak a glance or two in Elida's direction. He would also get a nasty look on his face whenever Dayvaun's name was mentioned.

I really think Marcus likes Elida. That bothers me. I know it shouldn't, seeing that I'm with Reggie now, but still. I liked Marcus first.

"Are you nervous about tonight?" I asked Elida.

"A little." She nodded.

"What's tonight?" Marcus asked.

"Her first date with Dayvaun."

Marcus rolled his eyes.

Yup, he's feeling her.

"Matter of fact, it's almost time for me to leave." She looked at her phone as she spoke.

My cell phone rang at that moment. I smiled as I saw it was Reggie. "Hello?"

"Hey, baby."

"What's up?"

"Nothing. Whatchu doing?"

"Chilling with Marcus and Elida."

"Oh okay. I'm about to come through, okay?"

"Fine with me. I'll see you soon!" We hung up. "Guys, Reggie is coming over!"

"Oh okay, well, I gotta go get ready." She stood up to leave. I shot a glance at Marcus, the scowl on his face more pronounced now.

Elida didn't seem to notice. "See you guys," she said, then she got up to go catch her Uber.

"Peace," Marcus said dully.

"See you!" My tone was cheery.

Elida

I left Shorty's house feeling nervous as hell. This was not only my first date with Dayvaun; it was my first date ever! I felt like I didn't know what to say, or what to do. I hoped my lack of experience didn't show. I almost cancelled when I got home, but I decided against it.

It was now or never.

I quickly showered and put on a cute outfit, then I took a Lyft to Dayvaun's house. I thanked the driver, then went to knock on Dayvaun's door. He had said he couldn't pick me up because he was rushing home from work, but if I met him at his house, he would drive us to our date and bring me back home.

He was supposed to be waiting outside when I got there, but I figured he was still getting ready.

"What's up, girl?" he said after opening the door. He was wearing a black wave cap, a royal blue T-shirt, black jeans, and black timbs. "You ready to go?"

"Yup!" I mustered up a smile while simultaneously attempting to disguise my eagerness, then we made our way to Dayvaun's car. We were driving for a little while, listening to trap music, then he pulled into a McDonald's parking lot.

Hmmm, I thought, but I didn't say anything.

We walked into the McDonalds and sat at a back table with lots of chairs.

"Um, you don't want a booth?" I was saying, but then an employee came up to us.

"Hey, are you guys going to order?" she said with attitude. She looked me up and down. "You can't just be sitting here without ordering anything. These seats are for customers only." She pointed to a sign that said the same for emphasis.

"Damn, bitch! Can we even get in the door first?" Dayvaun's voice was full of attitude. I took a step back, not liking the feeling of being in the middle of him and the employee.

Just then, a group of kids our age walked in.

"EYO!" Dayvaun said, a little too loudly, as he raised his hands in the air with a huge smile on his face. "We back here, my niggas!"

I stared as the other kids came to our table. There was a girl with them wearing a mini skirt so short it made me want to cover up. Her ass was hanging all out the back of it. There were also three guys. I didn't like the feeling of this at all. The guys sat down, and so did Dayvaun. The girl attempted to sit too, but Dayvaun stopped her.

"Uh uh. Come sit next to me." He said. My jaw dropped slightly as he smiled at her. She sat next to him, then shot me a glance as I was the only one still standing. Then Dayvaun put his arm around her, and she gave him a kiss on the lips.

"What the hell is going on here?" I demanded, feeling like my breath was being snatched from me.

Dayvaun looked up at me. "Why you ain't sitting down?" He gestured toward an empty seat next to one of his boys.

"Dayvaun, what are you doing?" I felt my heart fluttering.

"What do you mean what am I doing? Sit down." He gestured again.

"No…" I took a step back. "I thought we were here on a date."

"A date?" He looked confused.

"Yeah. We talked about it on the phone." I felt more and more stupid by the second.

"Oh, no. I'm not interested in dating you just yet. We're hanging out for now."

My ears grew hot as I took in the eyes of all of them staring at me.

Suddenly, I felt like I needed some air. I went outside to order another Lyft to take me back to Shorty's house. I didn't want to go home. Luckily, the driver was only four minutes away.

When I got inside, I looked back at the McDonalds to see if Dayvaun was going to come outside to see where I was, but he didn't. He was in there laughing it up with his friends, while the girl that kissed him was now sitting on his lap.

A tear attempted to escape from my eyes, but I blinked it back.

Shorty

Me, Reggie, and Marcus headed to Marcus' house to watch a movie after Elida left. I suggested it because my mom and Ronald would be home soon, and I didn't want them tripping. We heard a knock on the door about halfway through. Marcus pressed pause then went to go answer it, thinking it was the pizza guy.

It wasn't – it was Elida.

Almost as soon as Marcus opened the door, she collapsed into his arms.

Reggie and I jumped up to see what was going on.

"Elida, what is it?" Marcus held her as she sobbed. "What happened?" He looked up at us in confusion. "She said she was on her way back, so I figured the date was over."

After a moment, Elida calmed down, then told us the story. By the time she finished, we were all furious.

"That little punk ass, curly haired bastard," I spat.

Marcus had his arms around Elida, and he was still rubbing her back. "It's gonna be alright."

Elida broke away from him and went toward the door.

"Where are you going?" I asked. Marcus and Reggie looked confused.

"I gotta get home," she said. "My mom is gonna worry if I get back too late."

"You want me to order you an Uber?" said Marcus, pulling out his phone.

"No, I got it." She was already typing on her own phone.

"Elida, why don't you just stay with us for a while?" I asked. "You just got here."

"No, I need to go." When she was finished ordering her ride, she opened the door. "They are only two minutes away, so I'll wait on the porch."

Before anyone could say anything, she walked out and closed the door behind her.

We all stared at each other, wondering why she was leaving so abruptly, then Marcus opened the door to follow her.

Reggie and I watched as she approached the waiting vehicle. She and Marcus shared a few words, then they both got inside before the driver pulled off.

"Damn, Marcus got it bad," Reggie mused as we made our way back to the couch.

"Yeah," I said, feeling numb.

"What's wrong with you?" He studied my expression.

"Why is he always up under her?" I said before I could stop myself.

"What do you mean? Marcus and Elida?"

I nodded. "He acts like he's her man or something."

Reggie looked taken aback. "I mean... damn, Shorty. I thought that was your girl."

"She is."

"Why are you so worried about her and Marcus? If he likes her, so what? He would probably treat her way better than Dayvaun anyway."

I just stared at him.

He looked confused, then realization dawned. "Wow, Shorty. You have feelings for Marcus." He said it more as a statement than a question.

"So what if I do?"

His eyes narrowed. "You're supposed to be my girl."

"Well..."

"What the fuck am I here for, Shorty, if you want Marcus? I thought you wanted to be with me?"

"I did."

"How could you lead me on like that? I got feelings for you! I treat you right. I do anything I can for you. I thought you felt the same."

I just stared at him, my feelings of numbness continuing.

"Marcus don't want you, Shorty."

"Get the hell out."

"What?"

"It's over."

"Over? Shorty..." He reached out for me, but I pulled back.

"It's over, Reggie."

"Shorty, please."

"No. We're done."

He stared at me for a few moments, then he left. I waited until I was sure he was long gone, then I left too, locking Marcus' door behind me.

Marcus

I took the Lyft with Elida because I didn't want to let her go home alone in that condition.

On the way to her house, I tried to cheer her up.

"Light skinned niggas is played anyway, Ma."

That got a smile out of her.

"Come on," I grabbed her hand. "You'll be okay."

"Marcus..." Her voice trailed off.

"What is it?"

"I want to ask you a question, and you have to be honest with me."

"Okay." I was trying to figure out where she was going with this.

"Do you think I'm ugly?"

I couldn't believe my ears. "Ugly? Hell no!"

I said it so adamantly, this time she laughed.

"I guess I don't have to wonder if you're serious."

"Of course I'm serious. You're beautiful."

"You look damn good!" the driver said from the front seat.

We were so into our conversation, me and Elida almost forgot he was there. He was an older guy who looked to be in his forties.

"Thank you, Sir," Elida said.

"No problem. Every woman is beautiful in her own way, honey."

Elida gave me a strange look, then shot me a text. I checked it.

Isn't that what they say to ugly people?

We burst out laughing so hard I almost pissed myself.

The driver pulled up to Elida's house. "You feel better?" I asked.

She nodded. "I'll get over it."

"Okay, see you in school."

We had set up the ride so that the driver would bring me home after we dropped Elida off.

I waved at her as she was walking up to her house, then zoned out for a second.

Dave texted me. *Yo, I know shit been heavy lately. Wanna link up to talk about it?*

I contemplated his request.

It wasn't that I had anything against Dave; I just knew he rocked heavy with E and I didn't want to risk bumping into him.

Not tonight, but maybe we could link up after practice tomorrow.

Reggie

Fuck Shorty.
 She knew how I felt about her and still chose my boy over me. I really thought we had something. Guess not.

Marcus hit my line after I got home.

"What's good with you?" I answered. "You still with Elida?"

"Nah, I had the Lyft drop me off. When did you and Shorty leave? Dave just hit me a second ago too."

"After we broke up."

Marcus sounded shocked. "You and Shorty broke up? What the heck happened? Y'all seemed good when I left."

"I don't want to talk about it."

"You good though?"

"Yup. What was Dave talking about?"

"He said he wanted to link up to talk about what's been going on. I said we could get up after practice tomorrow."

"Cool."

"Yo Reg, you might as well spill the beans. What happened with you and Shorty for y'all to break up that quick?"

"Don't worry about it. Like I said, I'm good."

After me and Marcus hung up, all I could think about was Shorty. I wanted to call her, but I decided not to. She had already said her piece.

If she wanted Marcus, I was just gonna have to do me.

Elida

A couple of days passed since what happened with Dayvaun. Me and Marcus were sitting on my bed. No matter how hard I tried, I couldn't get what happened out of my mind.

"Don't even worry about him, Elida. He wasn't any good for you."

"I know, but it still hurts."

"I would never hurt you," he said softly.

"What do you mean by that?" He stared into my eyes, a strange expression in his. He opened his mouth to answer, but then Sammy opened my door and walked in.

"Marcus," he said. "My mom says you have to go home."

"Oh. Okay." He got up. We hugged, then he left.

I was laying there, staring at the ceiling for a while after he left.

Thoughts were just running through my mind. I was thinking about this system we are all caught up in. People live, people die, and the world goes on. But who makes the rules? Who says we have to go through life accepting it for the way it is? Why can't anybody change the way things are? A new poem came rushing out of me:

Break the Cycle

Gotta try to break the cycle
Can't let it get to me
Gotta beat it before it happens
That's all that matters to me
But what if it don't work?
What if I don't break the chain?
'Cause this shit is getting deep
It's the only thing on my brain
I wish that I could stop it
Make it all go away
Let's face it – that'll never happen
All my struggles are in vain
I wish I could make it stop
Put an end to all this pain
But I'd be a fool to waste my time
And watch my hopes get slain.

I hope next year is better than this year.

Shorty

Me and Reggie have been avoiding each other for the past few days in school. Elida keeps asking me why we broke up, but I won't tell her.

Part of me feels ashamed, but another part feels like she wouldn't understand anyway. Janie noticed the tension in our group.

"Hey," she said to me during one of the classes we had together. "What's been up with you?"

"Nothing. I'm surprised you showed up today." Janie had been skipping left and right.

"I figured since I made it this far, I might as well see if I can get to senior year."

"Of course you can. Just apply yourself."

She looked at me like she wanted to say something, but decided against it. "Did you and Reggie really break up?" she said instead.

My ears grew hot. "Who told you that?"

"Relax; it's just a rumor."

"From who, though?"

"It doesn't matter. Did you?"

I sighed. "Yes, we're broken up Janie."

"Do you want to talk about it?"

I looked at her. So much had changed between us, but Janie had that old look in her eyes. The look she had before all the bullshit started going down.

I wanted to trust her again.

"Let's hang out after school, and I'll tell you what happened."

Marcus

Me, Marcus, and Dave didn't get to have our conversation the other day because my dad came to pick me up from practice. I was surprised to see his car, but it wasn't like I could just leave him hanging. I turned back to Reggie and Dave.

"I'll have to get with y'all another time."

"Okay," Reggie said, then he waved at my Dad as we drove off.

Dave just looked disappointed.

"What's this about?" I asked Dad.

"I just wanted to do a little bonding."

"So you pop up on me at school?"

He paused. "I feel like you're drifting away from me, Marcus."

"Why do you say that?"

"I understand you're growing up and you have friends and school and basketball, but I miss how we used to hang out with just us two."

I thought about it for a second. "Me too."

"Are you mad I found another woman?"

His question caught me off guard, but I figured it would come sooner or later. "Not really. I mean, I guess it makes sense since Mom married that dude."

He drove in silence for a few more moments.

"Do you think you might want to meet Lisa?"

"I guess."

"Marcus, I don't want you to feel like I'm getting on you about your mother because her actions did hurt both of us, but sooner or later, you have to let it go."

"I understand that, Dad, but I just need time."

"Take your time. But don't take too long. Life is short, and you never know what's going to happen."

Reggie

We won the Championship game, and Coach gave both Marcus and Dave playing time like he did last year. Both of them got some points on the board.

"Keep it up, and you two will be ready for varsity next year!" he said.

Marcus and Dave looked at each other in surprise.

Rex approached us. "You fellas want to party tonight to celebrate the win?"

Dave spoke first. "Actually, we had other plans."

I opened my mouth to say something, but I didn't want to cause any issues since our relationship still wasn't fully back on track yet.

"A'ight man, your loss. Bethany says she misses you."

Dave smirked. "Tell her I miss her too."

Rex walked off.

"Why'd you turn down the party?" I asked when Rex left.

"I figured we needed to get our bond back tight before we continued branching out," Dave said.

Marcus gave him a weird look but didn't say anything.

"What did you have in mind?" I asked.

"Ron is actually throwing a party tonight."

Ron was another kid from our neighborhood. He lived on the far end of the complex. We didn't really hang there that much.

"When did you start hanging with Ron?" Marcus asked.

"I don't, really. But he invited us so I said we were down."

"A'ight, man," I said. We went home to get ready for the party.

We linked back up an hour later in front of Marcus' house. "Sorry I'm late," Marcus said when he finally came outside. "My dad was tripping, saying he didn't want me to go."

"Why not?" I asked.

Dave just gave him a weird look.

"He was saying we should have went with the team."

We started walking toward Ron's apartment, when Dave took a different direction.

"Where you going?" I asked.

"I wanted to hit this store right quick," he said.

Me and Marcus followed, while Dave walked. He cut through a side street, then went down the alley leading toward the store.

Me and Marcus walked down the alley too, wondering why he was moving so damn fast.

Then we heard a car screech behind us. Our heads whipped around.

A black Dodge Charger blocked the end of the alley we had come from, and E, Nino, and Dawan hopped out.

"What the fuck?" Marcus said.

We turned in the other direction, and saw Dave walking toward us, grabbing at his waist.

"What are you..."

I didn't need to finish my sentence, because Dave pulled out his gun and pointed it at Marcus as he continued to walk up.

Marcus' eyes widened. "Yo Dave, what the fuck man?"

My brain tried to assess this situation. *Dave set us up? Why?*

E also had his gun out on the other side of us. He spit on the ground as he approached, also pointing his gun at Marcus.

"Yo, this shit don't have to go down like this," I said.

"Shut the fuck up, Reg. You not the one we want," said E.

"It's this nigga right here." He poked the barrel into Marcus' chest, trying to scare him.

I couldn't tell what Marcus was feeling from his facial expression.

"Yo, whatever this is, it needs to be squashed right now. We was supposed to be boys. E, what the fuck is wrong with you?"

E pulled another gun out his waist and pointed it at me. So now there were two guns on Marcus, and one on me.

"What the fuck do y'all niggas want?" Marcus asked.

"Easy," Dave said. "We want…"

Before he could finish his sentence, a shot rang out.

To be continued…

Find out what happens next in the final installment of this series, Find You A Real One 2: A Friends to Lovers Romance.

Tanisha Stewart's Books

Even Me Series
Even Me
Even Me, The Sequel
Even Me, Full Circle

When Things Go Series
When Things Go Left
When Things Get Real
When Things Go Right

For My Good Series
For My Good: The Prequel
For My Good: My Baby Daddy Ain't Ish
For My Good: I Waited, He Cheated
For My Good: Torn Between The Two
For My Good: You Broke My Trust
For My Good: Better or Worse
For My Good: Love and Respect
Rick and Sharmeka: A BWWM Romance

Betrayed Series
Betrayed By My So-Called Friend
Betrayed By My So-Called Friend, Part 2
Betrayed 3: Camaiyah's Redemption
Betrayed Series: Special Edition

Phate Series
Phate: An Enemies to Lovers Romance
Phate 2: An Enemies to Lovers Romance
Leisha & Manuel: Love After Pain

The Real Ones Series
Find You A Real One: A Friends to Lovers Romance
Find You A Real One 2: A Friends to Lovers Romance

Standalones
A Husband, A Boyfriend, & a Side Dude
In Love With My Uber Driver
You Left Me At The Altar
Where. Is. Haseem?! A Romantic-Suspense Comedy
Caught Up With The 'Rona: An Urban Sci-Fi Thriller
#DOLO: An Awkward, Non-Romantic Journey Through Singlehood
December 21st: An Urban Supernatural Suspense

CPSIA information can be obtained
at www.ICGtesting.com
Printed in the USA
LVHW031802300821
696476LV00014B/298